Lessons Learned in Love

An inspirational romance

Milla Holt

Reinbok Limited

LONDON, UNITED KINGDOM

**Published by Reinbok Limited
Kemp House,
152 – 160 City Road,
London EC1V 2NX**

Book Layout © 2017 BookDesignTemplates.com
Editing by Krista Wagner

Lessons Learned in Love/ Milla Holt. -- 1st ed.
ISBN 978-1-913416-05-8

To my husband, who is my biggest
cheerleader,
and my amazing beta readers
Genevieve, Rachel, Deb, and
Elizabeth

contents

Chapter One

VANYA KLASSEN was used to being overshadowed, but her flamboyant dinner guest would have made even a peacock look drab. Although she had spent time with Maria Sifu before, Vanya struggled to rein in her inner fangirl. Maria was a legend in the international aid sector, and Vanya was in awe of all the woman had done.

Maria was dressed in her trademark flowing robes, her hair wrapped in a colorful turban. Although she was Caucasian, she had favored ethnic-influenced clothes ever since her marriage to a now-deceased Kenyan freedom fighter.

She took a dainty bite of her starter, poached lobster tail served with cauliflower and butter sauce, and smiled at Vanya. "It's wonderful to see what you've made of yourself since we last met. Public relations officer in your brother's company! I've always thought you were one of the more outstanding interns we've ever had at Development Action."

Vanya's face glowed under Maria's compliment. A decade ago, when Vanya was fresh out of high school, she'd spent three months interning at the international human rights organization Maria founded and still led. During those three months, Vanya had felt like she was making a difference for the first time in her life, even though she had mostly made photocopies and stuffed envelopes. Maria had let Vanya shadow her to meetings and strategy sessions, and Vanya loved every minute of it.

"That's really kind of you," Vanya said. "I've always—"

She was cut short as Maria waved down a passing waiter, who stopped and leaned forward. Maria jabbed a finger at her plate. "This cauliflower is overcooked. It's ruined the dish for me and I simply cannot eat it. Take the plate back and bring me one that's done properly."

The waiter apologized profusely and whisked the food away. Maria turned back to Vanya. "I'm sorry, you were saying?"

Vanya was taken aback. The guest of honor hated the food? The riot of butterflies in her own stomach had made it impossible for her to eat. She had picked this hotel because its conference and dining facilities were among the best in London. "I... I was just thanking you for your kind words. I really felt like I was helping make the world a better place when I interned with you."

Maria's smile was radiant. "Thank you. We do try our best. But you're doing wonderful work now with Nordic Wind and Acricaine. It will be an honor for my organization to partner with you."

Vanya smiled back, her mind flitting to the introductory speech she would be giving soon to the guests of tonight's black-tie charity banquet, announcing Maria's new collaboration with Nordic Wind. She'd rehearsed so many times that she knew every word by heart.

First, she would thank all the charity reps and members of the press for coming. She would say a few words about how her brother's pharmaceutical company would soon make its ground-breaking HIV treatment available at a huge discount to developing countries in deals brokered by Maria's organization. She would then invite Maria, the guest of honor, to give the keynote speech and take a few questions from the press.

The waiter came back and laid a fresh plate in front of Maria. She leaned forward and scrutinized the dish, then nodded at the waiter, who bowed and backed away.

Maria lifted a morsel of lobster to her mouth and chewed delicately. "This is actually edible." She looked up at Vanya. "I'm looking forward to working with you again. It will be so much fun, just like the old days."

She chuckled, and Vanya smiled. Before she could respond, a young woman stepped up to the table, clutching a hardcover copy of Maria's newly-published autobiography. The woman held the book forward. "I'm sorry to interrupt you, Mrs. Sifu, but would you mind signing this for me?"

Maria turned and stared at the young woman, her gray eyes stony despite the smile on her face. "It's Dame Maria, actually, since I received my OBE. It's important to pay attention to details like that. To whom shall I make out the autograph?"

Maria stretched out her hand and the young woman, now scarlet-faced, handed over the book and a pen and stammered out her name. Maria scrawled on the title page and gave the book back, barely glancing at the woman.

Vanya bit her lip as she watched the young woman scurry away. Maria was so famous now that she probably attracted a lot of autograph hunters, and it was doubtless irritating to be approached during a meal, but surely she could have been a bit more gracious.

Another woman came to the table. Vanya recognized her as one of

Maria's aides. She had a phone in her hand. Maria turned to Vanya with a sigh. "Seems I'm doomed not to eat my meal. Excuse me, dear. I need to take this call."

Vanya nodded, then checked her watch. It was only a few minutes until she had to give her speech. Just enough time to pop into the bathroom and pay for all the water she'd been nervously sipping. She excused herself and stood up, leaving Maria talking into the phone.

Vanya rehearsed her speech in her mind one more time as she headed for the restroom. She flushed when she was done and was just about to leave the restroom stall when she heard the bathroom door opening. Maria Sifu's voice floated in atop a cloud of lavender perfume. "Did you change my three o'clock appointment?"

"Yes, ma'am, I did." Vanya recognized the deferential tones of Maria's assistant.

Vanya hesitated with her hand on the lock of the stall door.

Maria was speaking again. "Excellent. Now to just get through with the rest of this evening. The press attendance seems good. I saw some faces I recognize from the BBC, ITV, and the *Guardian*. Anyone from outside the UK?"

The assistant said, "I spotted a lady from the Associated Press. I also saw people from the *Times*, the *Spectator* and Sky News. It's a great turnout."

"And I'm speaking after Vanya," Maria said. She sighed and uttered an expletive. "I can't wait to get it over with. One of the dullest evenings I've had in a long time."

Vanya's cheeks burned as she listened.

Maria's assistant spoke. "Not the most entertaining hostess, then?"

Maria chuckled. "Oh, please. She is the same tedious, insipid, average person she's always been. Mediocre on her best day. She would follow me around like a star-struck puppy and offer these pathetic little suggestions, and I'd have to smile as though they made any sense. The girl never held a single original thought in her head. The only reason I put up with her in the first place was because of her family name. Having her as an intern back then opened a lot of doors. You should know this by now. Access is the name of the game in this business. And the Klassen name comes with a lot of access."

"More access now since her brother owns Nordic Wind," the assistant said.

"Absolutely. Let me tell you, every NGO in town would give half their budget to get a foot in the door with Nordic Wind. I'm willing to put up with quite a few boring dinners with

Little Miss Humdrum to ally Development Action with Nordic Wind. At least the food today was halfway decent. Ah, well. I suppose we'd better go and get this over with."

The door swished open and closed and the bathroom was silent again. Vanya's hands were slick with a cold sweat as she fumbled with the sliding lock on the stall. She finally got it open and stepped out, staring at her own white-faced reflection in the mirror. Pain seared her heart even as her mind rebelled against believing what she had just heard. But that had been Maria's voice, and the air was still thick with her lavender perfume. *Tedious, insipid, average.* Her thoughts reeling, she grasped onto one thread: her speech. She needed to get back to the banquet room and give her speech. She ran water in the sink and washed her hands with robotic movements.

The girl never held a single original thought in her head. Her eyes filled up with tears. "Don't do this now," she whispered. She grabbed a paper towel, dampened it, and pressed it to her hot face. "I'll think about this later. Just get through the speech."

Her carefully-applied makeup was ruined, but there wasn't time to fix it now. Might as well just wash it off instead of appearing panda-eyed. *Mediocre on her best day.* Fresh tears threatened even as she splashed water on her face. This was the opinion Maria had held of her after all these years?

How was she supposed to go out and face a roomful of news media people and charity organization reps when she was in pieces inside? She dried her face and tried to fix her makeup, giving up when her hand wobbled too much.

Stepping out into the hall, she narrowly missed bumping into her sister-in-law, Nia, who was married to Vanya's brother Magnus and helped coordinate Nordic Wind's medicines access programs.

"There you are! I've been looking for you. It's time for your speech. They're all—" Nia stopped short, eyes widening as she looked at Vanya's face. "Are you okay?"

"I'm fine. Let's go."

Nia stared at her, then turned and led the way back into the banqueting hall. Vanya walked in, going past the tables where the assembled creme de la creme of the aid sector and the press sat in their evening finery.

She stepped up to the podium and stood at the lectern, taking several deep breaths. *You can do it. You can get through this.* A young man she recognized as the audio technician who worked for the conference facility fidgeted with the microphone.

An ocean of faces turned to face her. It was time. Vanya's vision centered on one face. Maria Sifu looked up, a slight smile on her face.

Suddenly, Vanya's mind flashed back ten years to a chat she'd once had with Maria.

Vanya, an overweight and pimply eighteen-year-old, in her only act of teen defiance, had rejected her mother's advice to attend an exclusive weight loss camp and instead took up the internship with Development Action.

Painfully shy and self-conscious, Vanya had been thrilled when Maria took notice of her, telling Vanya how much potential she had. "I expect great things from you," Maria had beamed.

Vanya had lived on that compliment for years, reminding herself that this woman, whom the whole world admired, had seen something special in her.

But now, that smile, those words, meant nothing. Less than nothing.

Vanya knew what Maria Sifu really thought of her. *Tedious, insipid and average. Mediocre on her best day.*

Vanya opened her mouth to speak, but no sound came out. Her lips trembled uncontrollably. The words she'd spent hours preparing and rehearsing fled from her mind, leaving a screaming void. Every eye was on her.

She looked at Maria again. The woman's smile resembled a smirk.

Vanya put a hand up to her mouth and a loud, ugly sob ripped out of her, amplified by the sound system until it echoed through the banqueting hall. The guests murmured, a nervous ripple spreading throughout the crowd.

Gasping for breath, tears streaming down her face, Vanya stumbled away from the microphone. She ignored the hands reaching out to her as she ran out of the room.

"Vanya, wait!"

It was Nia. In the antechamber outside the banqueting hall, Vanya turned around as her sister-in-law reached her and slipped an arm around her shoulder. "What's going on? Are you unwell?"

"I..."

"Come on, let's get out of here."

Vanya allowed Nia to lead her to a small break room, where Nia closed the door behind them. "I'm sure Magnus and Maria can handle the rest of the evening. Do you want to tell me what's going on?"

Tears rolled down Vanya's face. Nia put her arms around her, but that only made Vanya cry even more. Finally, she clawed back enough control to speak. "I'm sorry. I'm such a mess."

"What happened? Did you get some bad news?"

Vanya blew her nose. "I was in the bathroom and overheard Maria telling one of her aides what she really thinks about me. All this time I've thought of her as a mentor. Turns out she only wanted me around because of my family's connections."

Nia gasped. "That's disgusting."

Vanya's voice shook. "I can't work with her after this."

"None of us can. We should tell Magnus and maybe we can bow out of the collaboration."

Vanya shook her head. "It's too late. She's probably announcing it right now. You saw how the press were falling over her. If we pull out, thousands of people might lose out. I can't let that happen."

Nia looked at Vanya, her brown eyes searching her sister-in-law's face. "Are you sure? I'm pretty certain that Magnus would be happy to drop Maria and work with somebody else. That room is full of aid organization reps who would kill to partner up with us."

"No, let's not rock the boat. I'll just have to get used to it." Vanya's laugh was bitter. "She wouldn't be the first person who thinks I was born with a silver spoon in my mouth and had everything handed to me. Didn't you think the same thing when you first met me?"

Nia flinched and held her hands up. "Maybe, but I was a bit of an idiot when I met you and your brother, okay? Anyone who spends more than a few minutes with you knows what your heart is like and how hard you work and the incredible things you've achieved." Nia reached into her purse, found a tissue, and handed it to Vanya. "The problem is definitely with her and not with you. So, what are we going to do?"

Vanya sat with her shoulders slumped, wiping at her eyes. "Right now? If anyone asks, please tell them

I'm not feeling well and I'm going home."

Nia hugged Vanya. "I'll call and check on you later."

When her sister-in-law had left the room, Vanya jumped up and grabbed her purse. Nia and Magnus would manage the rest of the evening and make excuses for her. She couldn't stay here any longer. More importantly, she couldn't carry on working for Nordic Wind. Not when she'd be expected to collaborate with Maria.

Her job was over.

Chapter Two

ONSIDERING HE was about to make the presentation of his life, Tendo Halloran was surprised by how calm he felt. Time telescoped in and slowed to a crawl as he scanned the faces of the board members of Tymbrian Homes.

He saw a mix of expressions, from CEO and board chairman Karl Klassen's indifference to mild interest from the chief financial officer. His immediate boss and head of marketing, Suzy Huddleson, stared at him with hard features that occasionally cracked into a brittle smile when anyone else addressed her.

Tendo was giving this presentation against Suzy's wishes. She had shot down the ideas he was about to share, and she would vent her anger on him later. Unless he got the board to see things his way, which he had every intention of doing.

Karl shot his arm forward and glanced at his watch. "All right, gentlemen and ladies. Shall we begin?" The board members straightened up in their seats.

"We've been considering proposals about how to expand our market reach. In our management meeting two weeks ago, this young gentleman, Tendo Halloran, made a few intriguing points. I've asked him to address the board today and elaborate on those ideas." Karl made a welcoming gesture with his hand and all eyes turned to Tendo. "The floor is yours."

Tendo glanced at his notes, although he knew exactly what he was going to say. He breathed a quick prayer, then flashed a smile at his audience.

"Thank you, sir. Ladies and gentlemen of the board, I appreciate your time and attention, and I'll keep this brief. I've been in charge of content marketing with Tymbrian Homes for the past year. During that time, as I'm sure Suzy would attest—"

He glanced at her. She bared her teeth in the semblance of a smile. "During that time, we have seen a tremendous uptick in lead generation and conversions. However, we are merely scratching the surface of what is possible.

"Consumers are sick of being sold to. The hard sell marketing strategies of the past do not work anymore. These days, people are bombarded with sales messages and advertising everywhere they go. They are becoming more skeptical of these messages. They scroll past, switch off, block. So, how can we stand out in this crowded marketplace when everyone is shouting for attention?

"We stand out by doing something different. We build trust. Our messages need to give value to our potential customers. And we can do this by sharing useful information with them. Since we started a section on our company blog focused on homeowners, we've had a one hundred and twenty percent increase in customer inquiries.

"Our homeownership information pack has been downloaded by over ten thousand individuals, and there has been an increase in sales and new contracts."

The sales manager nodded emphatically, catching some glances from Karl and the other board members.

Tendo suppressed a smile, then paused for a moment until everyone's eyes turned back to him.

"If we achieved this with just one dedicated content manager, think of what could be done with a full department. Imagine an in-house brand publisher that creates not just blogs, but audio, text, and video content. Tymbrian Homes could become a thought leader in its industry space and the go-to information hub for our target audiences. With increased traffic will come increased trust and conversions into sales."

Karl leaned forward, fingers steepled, as he stared at Tendo. As Tendo continued speaking, he sensed that his points were hitting home. He outlined his vision for how Tymbrian Homes could expand its one-man content marketing office, which consisted of just him, into a fully-staffed in-house brand publisher.

"This department or team would be headed by a chief content officer who would report directly to the CEO. This person would create an editorial strategy and build up in-house media channels that create the sort of content that modern audiences trust and engage with." Ten minutes later, Tendo was done.

The board members looked at each other, and Karl smiled. "Thank you, Tendo. That was fascinating. Would you wait outside for a few minutes while we have a brief discussion? We may want you to come back in and field some questions."

His heart hammering, Tendo gathered up his papers and left the room. He released a slow breath as he stood in the hallway. His gut told him that the board members had liked what they'd heard. The big question was what would they do about it?

He hoped they would not only expand into brand publishing but put him in charge of the new venture. The buzz around the office was that the board was planning some big changes in the marketing department.

Working under Suzy for the past year had been an extreme trial of patience. Every one of those successes he'd outlined for the board had been achieved while she'd obstructed and hindered him.

She wanted nothing done for which she couldn't claim credit, and he knew the last thing she wanted was for him to step out from under her thumb and be free to show exactly what his ideas could do for the company if unhindered.

Well, in a few minutes he'd find out whether or not his gamble had paid off.

Tendo pulled his phone out of his pocket to check his messages, smiling at a one-word text from his mother Enid.

Well????

She'd been worried about the potential fallout of presenting to the board an idea his manager didn't like. She hadn't wanted him to take the risk, but Tendo hadn't come this far by playing it safe.

When you had a foreign name like his and came from the dregs of the state school system, you had to work extra hard for your resume to make an impression among the privately-educated Richards, Charlottes, Williams and Olivias.

And when they took a chance on you and called you up for an interview, you needed to stand out for more than your brown skin. Forget the extra mile: you had to run ten.

He walked toward the floor-to-ceiling windows at the end of the hallway. A spectacular view of London's cityscape spread out before him. These offices in Canary Wharf were less than two miles away from the deprived Tower Hamlets housing estate where he'd grown up with his mother. She had been a penniless Ugandan refugee when she had him.

Not for the first time, he was struck by the irony of how he was standing walking distance from the place where he and his mother had once been homeless, working for a company that built luxury homes.

He whirled around as the boardroom door opened. Suzy stepped out, holding a sheet of paper. Her red lips stretched in a smile as her eyes glinted.

"Well done, Tendo. You wowed the board with your presentation. They're all very impressed. Before they proceed with the rest of their discussions, Karl would like you to sign this." She held the paper out to him.

Tendo glanced at the handwritten lines, then back at Suzy. "What's this? A non-compete clause?"

"Yes. They want you to agree not to enter into another contract or trade that's in direct competition with Tymbrian Homes."

His pulse raced. Did this mean they thought his ideas were so good they didn't want him taking them off to any of their business rivals? Or were they getting ready to fire him and make sure he couldn't work anywhere else?

He lifted his eyes back to Suzy. "I'm not signing this unless it's attached to a new contract."

She blinked at him, the corner of her mouth lifting into a small smile. "No one can accuse you of lacking guts. I'll let them know."

She turned around and returned to the boardroom.

Chapter Three

"ARE YOU sure you want to eat that, dear? It will go straight to your hips."

Vanya's hand froze on the way to the second helping of garlic-roasted potatoes she'd been about to take. Her mother Jessica looked at her, head tilted, and went on speaking. "Being away from work has done your figure no favors, dear."

Vanya put her hands back on her lap. Her appetite for more potatoes, and indeed for the rest of her meal, was ruined. She lived in a one-story apartment that had been converted from what had once been the stables on her parents' estate. Being so close to the family home meant that Vanya ate dinner with her parents a couple of times a week. Or, more accurately, given Jessica's habit of commenting on Vanya's weight, she *didn't* eat dinner with her parents a couple of times a week.

Jessica, who had recently turned sixty, maintained her trim physique through a strict diet and exercise regimen. She rarely tired of telling her daughter she needed to work harder if she ever hoped to have the kind of body that turned heads and attracted potential marriage partners.

Karl, Vanya's father, dabbed his mouth with a folded napkin. "Speaking of this indefinite leave of yours, any idea when you'll be returning to Nordic Wind?"

Vanya shifted in her seat. This was exactly the conversation she didn't want to have. Since her spectacular meltdown three weeks ago, she'd been taking time off work. In addition to wanting to avoid meeting Maria, she couldn't stand the thought of facing everyone who'd seen her at the gala. It was much easier to hang out at home with the occasional visit to her brothers.

"I don't know," she said, picking at a loose thread on the edge of her sleeve.

When her brother Magnus had heard about Maria's nasty comments, he'd wanted to confront the woman, but Vanya had begged him not to. The two-year collaboration with Development Action would go forward. Vanya knew she needed to put on her big girl pants, stop hiding, and face up to the fact that there would always be two-faced hypocrites who'd smile at her while whispering behind her back.

Maria's words echoed in her head. *She is the same tedious, insipid, average girl I remember... At the time she worked for me she was strictly average. Mediocre on her best day.* Tears pricked her eyes, and she hid them by taking a sip of water from a large glass.

Karl turned his gray eyes on Vanya. "I won't pry into what's been going on, but if you're interested in trying something new, I've got something in the works at Tymbrian Homes, and I'd appreciate your help."

"Okay," Vanya said, keeping her tone neutral. She'd worked at Tymbrian Homes for a couple of years before she'd joined Nordic Wind. "What's going on?"

"We're opening a new department. From what I understand, it's going to be content marketing on steroids. Brand publishing is the new buzzword."

Vanya sat up. "You're getting into brand publishing? That's a great idea."

Karl's mouth tilted upwards. "Quite. The board has been studying a number of proposals to expand our market and we've decided to go ahead in this direction. I've got the file on the desk in my study. Why don't you have a look and see if that's something you'd like to be involved in?"

"Involved in what way?"

"Heading up the department."

Warmth flooded Vanya's body. "Really? I'll go read the proposal."

She found the file easily and sat down at her father's desk. As she paged through the document, her excitement grew. The ideas for the new department were brilliant. There was so much she could do here. And head a whole department? Her father had never given her that level of responsibility before. In her last stint at Tymbrian Homes, she'd felt like a glorified executive assistant.

But the insecurities stoked by Maria's words still niggled. Apart from that internship at Development Action, Vanya had only ever worked for family members: first with her father's companies, then with her brother. This was just another family job, unearned and possibly undeserved. What if there were people like Maria who would think she was a mediocre and average person who only got a top management position because her daddy owned the company?

Vanya chewed her lip. There would always be whispers behind her back. But what was the alternative? Find another job outside her family's businesses? Give up work and follow in her mother's footsteps, spending her days between beauty treatments and appointments with a personal trainer? No, she wanted to take on Karl's offer. She could bring value to the business and prove to herself she could make a difference. Karl was her father, but he cared about the bottom line. He wouldn't have offered her a job if he didn't think she could handle it.

But what about Nordic Wind? She frowned. Magnus could easily find somebody to take care of the work she'd been handling. Nothing seemed to have gone drastically wrong there in the three weeks she'd been gone. The truth was, she was completely replaceable. Not a nice thought after she'd been working there for three years.

She clutched the folder and stood up. This was a project she could take charge of and one that would highlight her capabilities. Her mind made up, she went toward the patio to find her father.

Chapter Four

TENDO WONDERED how long he could stand the tension. In the weeks since he'd presented his idea to the board and refused to sign the non-compete clause, he'd heard nothing.

Suzy had avoided speaking to him apart from the bare minimum of communication, listening with little comment to his updates at the weekly team meetings. He preferred it that way rather than having her micromanaging his work, but her silence unnerved him. What did she know that he didn't?

As the weeks stretched into one month and crept up to two, Tendo grew certain the board had decided to shelve the idea. Oh, well, he'd known it was a gamble to speak to them. His contract was almost up; perhaps it was time to start looking for other opportunities.

His head jerked up as Suzy stepped in from the hallway, pausing in the doorway of the office he shared with a handful of other people from her marketing department.

"Tendo, could I have a word, please?"

He stood up from his desk and walked after her, aware of the gazes that followed him. This was the first time in almost two months he'd spoken to his line manager beyond the most perfunctory exchanges.

They entered her office and she spoke over her shoulder as she walked round to her desk. "Close the door behind you, please, and take a seat."

Tendo did as she asked, settling on the edge of an upright chair. She leaned her elbows against her desk, resting her chin on her latticed fingers. For a long moment, she stared at him. He met her gray eyes without speaking. Trust Suzy to make everything a little power game. Well, he wasn't playing.

Finally, she leaned back. "The board loved the presentation you gave them. So much so that they are running with your idea to expand their content marketing outreach."

Tendo knew his mouth was hanging open. Every fiber in his body wanted to whoop with excitement, but he held himself back, pressing his lips together with an effort. He nodded because he didn't trust his voice to hold steady.

"They are creating a brand publishing department, as you

suggested, and you will be moving from my marketing department to work there." She gestured a smooth manicured hand to a file in the middle of her desk. "This is your new contract."

She watched his face, as though waiting for him to say something. He asked, "So, I'll be leading the department?"

Suzy's lips parted in a smile. That made Tendo uneasy. "I didn't say you'd be leading the department. It's a sideways move for you. You'll work under a new department manager. Karl's bringing in his daughter Vanya to take the lead on this."

A numbness started in Tendo's core and spread through his body. His face must have mirrored the shock, because Suzy's eyes narrowed and she pouted in sympathy as fake as the potted orchid on her windowsill. "Oh, I'm sorry. Did you think you were going to be the brand publishing manager? No, you'll be answering to Vanya Klassen. She's a lovely girl. We went to the same school, you know, although she was a couple of years behind me. We were on the tennis team together. We were all afraid of her topspin serve."

Tendo's hands balled into fists. He forced them to relax. "May I have a look at the contract?"

"Of course. Here you go." She slid it across to him, and he schooled his features to remain impassive as he leafed through the document. As Suzy had said, he would be reporting to the head of brand publishing. His proposed salary was almost twice what he was getting now, "plus annual performance bonus." His heart rate quickened. An income boost like this meant he could do a lot more for his mother, maybe help her move away from the shady neighborhood where she still lived.

Suzy spoke again. "I should draw your attention to the last page. If you do take the job, they'll want you to sign a non-compete clause. You wanted to see it attached to a contract, if I remember correctly."

Tendo swallowed hard. Suzy wasn't even pretending not to enjoy this. She grinned at him like a cat toying with a helpless mouse. He focused on the words that swam in front of his eyes, grasping for control. *Think, Tendo.*

It wasn't the job he'd wanted, but it was an excellent offer. Taking it and signing that non-compete clause meant that if he left, he would be prevented from working with another company in the same space for two years. But he could easily transfer his skills into any number of industries. Although maybe not at this level of pay.

He turned back to the front page and scanned the payment and benefits package. Those were the golden handcuffs. He wasn't rising up in the company, but at least he was getting paid. He wondered what this Vanya Klassen was like. She would probably be just like her school friend Suzy: pampered and unqualified. Hopefully she wouldn't get in his way.

Suzy clicked her tongue, making a "tsk" noise. "Poor Tendo. You'll have to work with another woman. I do hope your ego can take it."

He stared at her for a moment, then turned his eyes back to the contract. If she thought she was humiliating him, she had no clue about what made him tick. There was nothing humiliating about paying his mortgage and making sure his mother would never live in poverty again. He pulled a pen out of his shirt pocket, uncapped it, and scrawled his signature on the dotted line before he flipped over to the second copy and signed that as well.

He stood up and left Suzy's office without a backward glance.

Chapter Five

VANYA STOOD in the middle of her new office at Tymbrian Homes. She ran her fingers along the edge of her bow-fronted desk and looked around the room. This was going to be her new start, the place where she made her mark.

Magnus had been disappointed but not surprised when she'd told him she was not going back to his company. As she'd suspected, it had been depressingly easy to replace her at Nordic Wind. She frowned. Of course she didn't want to leave her brother in the lurch, and it was great that his business would carry on seamlessly. But it did nothing for her self-esteem to see the company moving along without missing a beat. Hopefully she'd be less forgettable here.

She sat down at her desk. She couldn't use her computer until the IT guys set it up. In the meantime, she had asked her PA to arrange a meeting with the department's only other employee so far. One of her first tasks would be to hire new staff members.

Vanya pulled out the proposal Karl had given her, now dog-eared after the number of times she had thumbed through it to glean ideas for her new department.

"Vanya, darling, there you are."

Vanya stood up as Suzy strode into the office, her figure displayed to perfection in a tight gray pencil skirt and red silk blouse. Suzy came close enough to exchange air kisses, then stood back. "It's wonderful to have you here. Are you getting settled in?"

Vanya smiled. "I'm trying to get my head around what to do first. I'll be meeting with my deputy manager in a minute."

Suzy quirked an eyebrow and her lips twisted in a smile. "Ah, you're about to meet Tendo Halloran. He used to work for me, you know."

Vanya blinked. "He did?"

"Mm hmm. In fact, that's why I popped in here. I wanted to give you a little heads-up." Suzy stepped forward and dropped her voice. "You want to keep an eye on that one. He's smart and good at what he does, but I don't think he likes having to defer to a female boss. You'll need to be confident and show him you're in charge. In fact, I wouldn't be surprised if he were after your job."

Both women glanced up at the sound of a knock on the door. A tall dark-skinned man stood there. His gaze flicked to Suzy before it turned toward Vanya. "Good morning. I'm Tendo Halloran. I understand you wanted me to stop by."

Heat crept up Vanya's neck and into her cheeks. Had he overheard anything Suzy had said? She walked forward, hand extended. "Hi, I'm Vanya. Please come in."

He held her hand briefly and stepped into her office. Suzy smirked. "Well, I'll be off, then, and let you two get acquainted. Good luck on your first day, Vanya. Congratulations once again, Tendo, on your, um... transfer."

Tendo answered Suzy with a curt nod. He waited until she had left the room, then sat in an armchair next to a low table in response to Vanya's gesture.

"Tendo... that's a name I haven't come across before."

"It's quite a common name where my mother comes from. She tells me it means 'praise'."

"Oh, I see. That's nice. Um, right. Well, thanks for coming." She went to her desk and picked up the department proposal she'd been reading. "I'm really excited about getting started with all this. I understand you've been content manager here for the last year?"

He nodded. "That's right."

"The board wants us to hit the ground running, and we've got a lot to do." She held up the proposal. "They gave me this, which is a useful roadmap for what we need to do to get started. It would be great if you could read it so we're on the same page before we have our first proper brainstorming meeting later today."

Vanya lay the proposal on the table next to him. He picked the document up slowly. "Sorry about all the marks and highlights on it," she said. "As soon as the IT guys set me up, I'll print out a fresh copy, but I'd like you to get familiar with it straight away."

He looked up at her, his lips twisting in a smile that didn't quite reach his brown eyes. "Actually, I'm already rather familiar with this proposal. I wrote it."

Heat rushed to Vanya's face in a painful flood. "You... what? Oh, you wrote it?" She reached out to take the proposal back, then withdrew her hand. Her chest tightened. "I'm sorry, I... no one told me. Um, okay."

She went back to her desk. He leaned back in the chair and crossed his legs, watching her. She was sure her face was flaming red. Of course he'd written it. He'd been content manager here for a while, and someone had to have put this document together for the board. She'd assumed they'd hired a consultant. Why hadn't it occurred to her that someone within the company had written this? She was about to pretend to busy herself with her computer, then remembered it wasn't set up yet.

She turned back to look at him, struggling to keep a professional tone. "That proposal was excellent work. Shall we meet in about an hour and draw up a plan of what our next steps are going to be?"

He stood up. "An hour's fine. I'll see you back here." He set the proposal back on the table and smiled at her again. "I'll let you keep your copy."

She watched him walk out, then sank into her chair with a groan, slapping her forehead with the palm of her hand. She'd been about to lecture him on a strategy that he'd written himself. How much more awkward could it get? If this Tendo was smart and creative enough to have drawn up a plan like this, why wasn't he the one in charge of the department? Her stomach tightened. He was probably thinking the same thing.

Dread settled in the pit of her stomach like a ball of lead. She was going to be managing someone who could do her job better than she did. She'd taken this position because she wanted to run away from a huge blow to her ego. But even here she couldn't escape the fact that there would be people who thought she didn't deserve her role. She recalled Tendo's face, his smirk as he'd told her that he would leave her copy of the proposal behind. What was it going to be like to work with him if he didn't respect her authority? *God, help me!* She prayed silently. She was going to need all the help she could get.

Chapter Six

ENDO SUPPRESSED a smile as he walked up to his desk. Perhaps it was petty, but he'd enjoyed that encounter with his new boss. The look on Vanya's face when he'd told her he was the one who'd written that proposal was worth the humiliation Suzy had tried to put him through.

He'd almost felt sorry for Vanya as he'd watched her squirm. Almost, but not quite. In his experience, the only thing worse than an overbearing boss was an insecure one. And despite her impeccable designer wardrobe, family pedigree, and big job title, Miss Vanya Klassen came across as very insecure.

Perhaps her age had something to do with it. She was a lot younger than he'd been expecting. He sensed a softness about her that was in contrast to the hard edge of his former manager. Whatever. He wasn't interested in playing office politics or buttering up his boss. All he wanted to do was do his work well, get fairly compensated, and move on up the career ladder.

He opened his computer to a long-form blog post he'd been editing and tuned his mind to focus on his work. A chime from his phone shattered his concentration. He glanced at the screen. It was a text message from a number he didn't recognize. He was about to delete it when the words "your mother" snagged his eyes. He opened it.

This is a friend of your mother Enid. Somebody put a brick through her window and she's at the hospital.

Tendo jumped to his feet, his heart hammering while heat flared in his body. He clenched his teeth. "Somebody?" He had a good idea who'd done this. He punched in his mother's number. Enid answered, her voice sounding strained. "Tendo. How are you?"

"Mum, are you okay? I just got a message telling me you're in the hospital."

"I'm all right. They say I have a mild concussion."

"What happened?"

"Somebody threw a brick into the window. It didn't hit me, but when it happened I was startled and I tripped and hit my head on the table."

Tendo's hands shook. "Did you see who did it?"

There was a moment's silence at the other end of the line. Then, "No."

Enid may not have seen who had attacked her house, but Tendo knew she had a pretty good idea who it was. For the past year and a half, she'd been the target of bullying and harassment from a family who occupied three houses on her council estate. It had started when she'd asked her next door neighbor not to dump their garden waste over the fence into her backyard. The neighbor had carried on, and Enid lodged a complaint with the council.

That's when the neighbor's family members, who also lived on the estate, had gotten into the act. Stares and taunts had escalated into Enid's bins being upended, rubbish being strewn over her front lawn, and her house being egged. Her car had been keyed and someone had pushed nails into her tires. Two weeks ago, somebody had stuffed a potato into her muffler.

And now one of them had thrown a brick through her window.

"Are you okay? What does the doctor say?"

"They said I'm okay to leave, as long as someone is with me. I'm just waiting for my friend Heather to pick me up and take me back home."

Tendo gritted his teeth. "You're not going back to that house. I'm bringing you to my place. Which hospital are you in?" She told him and he said, "I'll be there as soon as I can."

He ended the call and took a moment to control his breathing. He wanted to go down to that miserable housing estate and pulverize every one of those lowlifes who were behind this. He could call the police, but past experiences told him that there wouldn't be much they could do. The Kelly family would stick together and nobody else on the estate would admit to having seen anything. They were all afraid of facing the same sort of abuse from the Kellys, who ran the street.

Tendo channeled his rage into action. The best thing to do was get his mother out of there and leave that sink estate to the rabble who wanted to drag it down even further. He'd need to ask his new boss for permission to take the rest of the day off. Not the best impression to make on her first day, but right now, he didn't care. His priority was to get his mother somewhere safe.

He went to Vanya's office and knocked on the door frame. She glanced up at him and he spoke quickly. "A family emergency has just come up. I hate to ask, but I'll need to take the rest of the morning off."

Her blue eyes grew wide and she nodded. "Of course. Take the whole day if you need to."

"Thank you."

He turned to go, and she spoke again. "I hope everything will be okay."

He paused, surprised by the concern on her face. She looked as though she meant what she said. He thanked her and stopped by his office to grab his jacket.

Tendo's mother smiled when he arrived at the hospital to pick her up. She had a bump on her head the size of a goose egg, but appeared otherwise unhurt. "You didn't need to come. Heather could have given me a ride."

He hugged her. "I had to come and make sure you actually went to my place instead of going back to Wood

Green." He scanned her face. "Are you sure you're okay?"

"The doctor said I'll be fine. It's a mild concussion, so she said I need to take it easy, and somebody should be with me for the next twenty-four hours. Heather said she could—"

"You'll stay with me," Tendo said firmly. "And we're going to talk to the council and demand that they do something about this. Let's go home." He placed his hand under her elbow as she stood up. She was tiny, her head only coming up to his chest. She was certainly no match for that gang of brutish louts who persisted in bullying her.

The old Tendo would have retaliated against his mother's bullies, going against them with every weapon and tactic he could muster, not thinking about the consequences. But his stepfather, the gentle Irishman whose surname he had taken as his own, had taught Tendo that revenge led nowhere.

"Use your head, lad," Patrick Halloran would tell his then-teenaged stepson whenever Tendo had tussled with bullies around the neighborhood or on the school playground. "You've got brains. You can get yourself an education and make a life for yourself that those idiots can only dream of. God will handle them in His own time."

A sudden mist clouded Tendo's vision as he thought of his stepfather. That was one of the major bones he had to pick with God. He was grateful to God for bringing Patrick into his and Enid's life.

But why did Patrick have to die so soon?

Enid kept up a brave front, but Tendo knew that she missed her husband. Well, now it was Tendo's job to be there for her and keep her safe from those louts.

His determination to take care of his mother was why he'd driven himself so relentlessly in his career, burying himself in work and study that crowded out any other distractions. Thankfully, all the hard work was bearing fruit.

He had a nice new pay raise now, which meant he could contribute more and help his mother find somewhere better to live. If he had anything to do with it, Enid was never going back to that miserable estate.

He led her to his car and started the drive back to his apartment.

Chapter Seven

A FEW DAYS later, Vanya sighed and dropped her pen on her notepad as the last job applicant of the day walked out of the conference room. She took a large sip from her water bottle to ease her parched throat.

After a long day of interviewing candidates for in-house copywriting and social media management jobs, there was still more work to do. She needed to decide on whom to hire before she went home tonight.

Tendo sat next to her, making notes in his own notepad with precise cursive letters. How did he manage to look—and smell—so fresh at the end of a long day? His crisp white business shirt looked as freshly laundered as it had in the morning, his rolled-up sleeves and loosened tie the only concessions to the length of time they'd spent in here working.

Carrie, the human resource manager, pulled together her documents as she smiled at Vanya. "That was a varied bunch! I'll let you two carry on with your deliberations and wait for you to forward the details of whomever you pick."

Vanya smiled back. "Thank you. Hopefully, that will be soon."

Carrie left the room and Vanya stood up to stretch her muscles. "Shall we start with the lead copywriter's job?"

Tendo looked up from his notes. "Who do you think stood out?"

"It's a strong shortlist, but I'm leaning toward the second candidate, Pamela Martin."

Tendo's eyebrows rose. "That's interesting. I thought Adam Brent was much stronger. He interviewed well, and he's got the most experience out of all of them."

Vanya's stomach knotted up. Of course Tendo was going to disagree. She always felt as though she needed to justify her decisions to him. It was just that cool vibe he gave off, that quirk of the eyebrow that urged her to explain herself, to prove that her thought process made sense.

She went back to her seat and shuffled through the papers. "Why don't we take a closer look at their applications? Was there anyone else who stood out apart from these two?"

Tendo looked at his own stack of papers, then back at Vanya. "I also liked Anila Gupta. She'd be my second choice after Adam. I'd rate Pamela as number three."

"Anila was good, but she said she wouldn't be able to start work for at least two months. We need somebody straight away. Anyone else?"

Tendo shook his head. "If Anila's out, that leaves Pamela and Adam. Like I said, Adam's resume is solid. He's been a copywriter for two years and he's worked for two leading industry names. His academic credentials are the strongest out of all of them."

Vanya recalled Adam. He seemed like a blond, blue-eyed version of Tendo. Confidence seeped out of every pore; he'd had no problems answering any of the questions or talking about how he was the best person for the job. No wonder Tendo liked him. The two of them were like two peas in a pod. But despite Adam's obvious strong points, something about Pamela had grabbed Vanya.

She pulled out Pamela's resume. As she looked it over again, it suddenly hit her why she liked Pamela. "I agree that Adam is strong, but have a look at Pamela's resume again."

When Tendo had the CV in front of him, Vanya said, "It's true that Pamela doesn't have as much of a professional track record as Adam does, but she's been running a personal blog for over five years. She's built up enough traffic to generate almost one thousand visitors a day. She also has a related YouTube channel that has almost a hundred thousand subscribers. And this is just what she's done in her free time."

Vanya held the resume up and looked at Tendo. "She's passionate about creating content. She loves it so much that she does it for fun, and does it well enough to build a following that a lot of small businesses would pay good money to get. Adam has the qualifications and the professional track record, but I think Pamela's got this in her blood. And when we asked how she might expand our content outreach, Adam's answers were generic. He talked about what everyone else is doing. But Pamela had some very creative ideas; she seemed to have a natural instinct about how to engage our audiences."

Tendo crossed his arms. "Some of her suggestions were slightly hare-brained."

"A couple might have been rather unorthodox, but there's potential in her ideas about podcasting and influencer marketing."

Tendo inclined his head. "Those were interesting ideas. But I think that, on balance, Adam would be a better choice." He leveled his gaze at her, and she read a challenge in his eyes.

She stood up again and crossed the room, more to have something to do than because she needed to. She turned around and faced him. "I hear what you're saying, and Adam is a safe and sensible choice, but I'm going to go with my gut. I'll ask Carrie to offer Pamela the job. If she's unable to take it, we'll contact Adam."

Tendo shrugged. Vanya picked up another list of job applicants. "Let's talk about the social media marketing role. What did you think?"

The afternoon wore on as they discussed who would be best for which role. Tendo didn't want to take a break, and Vanya decided to push on and get it all over with.

By the time they were done, she was exhausted. Tendo had opposed her views on three different candidates. Each time, he'd favored the people with more experience and other professional credentials, while she'd been drawn to those who she thought had more potential or what she called a "creative spark." But although she'd disagreed with him, she ended up agreeing to offer jobs to most of his preferred candidates. Pamela was the only one she insisted on hiring over his objections.

But she was already second-guessing her choice. What if she was wrong and she was hiring a substandard candidate? Maybe it was a sign that she was a mediocre boss surrounding herself with mediocrity.

Tendo stood up with his stack of files. "If we're done here, please excuse me."

She pushed her hair back from her face and looked up at him. "Thanks for your input. We covered a lot of ground, and hopefully we'll have a full team in just a couple of weeks."

"We haven't yet chosen a videographer. Did you decide whether you want to hire an in-house person or use an outside agency?"

Vanya's mind protested at the thought of making another major decision today. "Let's discuss that first thing on Monday. It will depend on several issues, not least of all the budget we can spare."

"Okay. See you on Monday."

She watched him leave the meeting room. Her mind wandered to speculations about how he was going to spend his weekend. Was he married? Did he have a girlfriend? He probably had more exciting plans lined up than she did.

She'd promised her mother to attend some sort of get together she was having tomorrow afternoon. It would probably be as stiff and boring as all her mother's parties were, but at least it would take her mind off a growing sense that she was failing at work.

Ever since her faux pas about Tendo being the author of the proposal she'd waved in his face, she'd never felt like she'd recovered her footing. She imagined he was weighing her and finding her wanting. His questioning her choices about who to hire just fueled her insecurity.

She went to her office and pulled open a drawer, dropping in her files. No more thinking about this until next week. She'd try to keep her mind off it all until then. There would be plenty more time to worry about failing at her job.

Chapter Eight

ER MOTHER'S party was going exactly how Vanya had expected. The house was full of well-dressed society names who had little to say of any interest to Vanya once they got past the initial chitchat. But Jessica insisted that Vanya show up, and it was hard to avoid these parties when she lived on her parents' property.

Vanya wished she'd been like her brothers who had long ago decided that they didn't want to attend any of Jessica's society events. First Ragnar and then Magnus had refused to attend until their mother had stopped asking. Vanya probably ought to have moved away as well and gotten an apartment of her own.

Could haves and should haves wouldn't help her now, though. Today she was still on the hook, and Jessica expected her to make an appearance and help with the hostessing duties. Hired caterers handed round drinks and canapes, so Vanya couldn't disappear into the kitchen to pretend her help was needed there.

She never drank alcohol, so she couldn't rely on that crutch to make the people here seem more interesting than they actually were. She sat in a corner of the lounge sipping a glass of soda water and waiting until she could claim fatigue and retreat to her place.

Jessica walked into the room and called out in her clear bell-like tones. "Vanya, there you are. Come over here, sweetheart. There's someone you need to say hello to."

Vanya took a couple of steps forward and her heart thumped when she saw who was standing next to her mother. Derek Coleman-Baines. Jessica had mentioned he was back in town, but she hadn't expected to see him here today.

She'd had a huge crush on him back in her high school days, but hadn't seen him in years, since he'd moved to the US. Her hand flew to her hair before she could stop it, and she was relieved that she'd taken her mother's advice and stopped at the salon today to get her blond hair cut and styled.

Jessica said, "Here she is, Derek. You two find a quiet corner and chat and I'll just go and have a word with Sir Giles over there."

Vanya hoped her makeup was hiding her reddening face after her mother's blatant ploy to push her and Derek together. He grinned, flashing those deep dimples that had made her and her classmates giggle when they'd meet him at tennis tournaments. He'd been a heart-throb as a teenager, but Derek at thirty was even more gorgeous.

"Little Vanya, look at you! It's been ages. How are you?"

"Great, thank you. How are you? I didn't realize you were in the UK."

"I am, and I've moved back to stay. Why don't you tell me what you've been up to? Did I hear that you were working with your brother's drug company? Wish I'd invested there when I had the chance. I'd have made a killing." He chuckled, showing off those dimples again.

"I was working there until last month. I'm working with my father right now, at Tymbrian Homes. What about you?"

"Oh, this and that." He steered her toward where she'd been sitting, and she settled back down, staring into his blue eyes. He carried on speaking. "I've invested in a bit of property and I've been managing Mother's country estate, of course. But a few years ago, I started a videography company and that's been doing quite well. We've won a few industry awards for our short films."

Vanya's interest was piqued over and above Derek's dimples. "Videography? What sort of films do you make?"

"Whatever we're hired to do. We've done a few documentaries and some experimental shorts."

"Do you by any chance take on work for corporate clients? Like companies who want video content?"

Derek smiled. "Interesting you say that. I was just talking to your father about how we are branching out in that direction. Since I've moved operations back to the UK, I've been sending out feelers. And your father said that you might be interested in hiring a videographer."

Vanya tilted her head. "I just might. Why don't you tell me a bit more about these experimental films you've done."

She listened as Derek told several anecdotes about his projects, including amusing stories of going to the Cannes Film Festival to show a couple of his experimental short films and hobnob with famous people in the movie industry.

"Have you ever been to Cannes?" he asked.

"Never. Mum went a couple of years ago, but I didn't go with her."

"You'd fit right in. It's a city for the glamorous."

Vanya's cheeks warmed up. Back in school, her pimply chubby-thighed self would have swooned to death to hear Derek call her glamorous. Right now, she did a semi-swoon inside as she noticed the open admiration in his eyes.

"So, why didn't you go to Cannes with your mother?" he asked.

Vanya shrugged. "I was busy with work. Magnus's company was about to go public, and we had to make an unscheduled trip to Africa. It was a crazy time, so there wasn't really time to go on holiday."

"You always were a serious little bookworm," Derek said. "My friends and I all used to wonder what you did besides study and play tennis. Do you still play, by the way?"

"When I get the chance. How about you?"

"Yes, I do. We ought to get together sometime." He looked deep into her eyes. "I'm serious. I'd like to see whether your topspin serve still delivers the goods."

Vanya turned her eyes down and took a sip of her soda water. Was he flirting with her?

"Do you still play at the Copman Heath Tennis Club?" He pulled out his phone. "Let me have your number. Perhaps we can meet for a match next week."

She gave him her phone number and he tapped it into his smart phone. "Looks like you need a refill. What are you having?"

"Soda water."

"What, nothing more adventurous?" He leaned forward and winked. "Your parents don't have to know. And besides, you're not at St. Cuthbert's anymore."

"I'm fine, thanks. I never drink alcohol."

His eyebrows flew up. "What, never? Oh, right, I remember you were religious."

"I am religious, but it's not just that. I never developed the taste for it."

"Fair enough." Derek looked up and caught the attention of a waiter who was hovering nearby with a tray. "Excuse me. Two soda waters, please." He turned back to her and flashed those dimples again. Suddenly, Vanya was in no hurry to leave her mother's party.

Chapter Nine

ENDO GOT to his desk on Monday morning to find a memo from Vanya's PA telling him that the previously-scheduled 8:30 meeting had been pushed to nine o'clock. Tendo busied himself checking his emails and starting on a list of projects the new copywriter would need to tackle. He hoped Vanya's pick would be up to the job. She would need to be exceptionally productive to keep up with the pace he was planning.

At nine o'clock, he closed his file and walked the few steps down the hallway to Vanya's office. There was laughter coming from inside. Vanya wasn't alone. A dark-haired man with movie star looks and an expensive suit lounged in an armchair. He and Vanya had clearly been enjoying a joke, because the last remnants of a smile lingered on her lips as she turned to face Tendo.

"Good morning. I'd like you to meet Derek Coleman-Baines. His company will be creating video content for us."

Tendo stopped short. When had this been settled? He and Vanya were still supposed to work out whether they wanted to hire a videographer or contract out the work. He accepted the hand Derek extended.

"Hi, Tendo. Good to meet you." Derek turned back to Vanya. "I'll tell you later what became of Gregory's yacht. All I'll say at the moment is it involved a llama and a trapeze artist."

Vanya giggled and Tendo got the picture. These two had something else going on. Whatever. It wasn't any of his business what she did in her private life. All that mattered was whether this fellow could do his job.

Vanya gestured toward the other armchair. "Please have a seat, Tendo. I wanted us to talk about our video content for Tymbrian Homes' content channels." She flipped through some pages in her planner. "The company will soon be breaking ground on the St. Mary Heath estate, and it would be great if we were able to launch our upgraded content hub at the same time. That gives us about three months, which is perfect, because I like to work in twelve-week sprints."

Tendo had opened his own planner as she spoke, and uncapped his pen. "So, we need to figure out what that video content will be."

"Exactly. Derek has some ideas, and I know that you also had several thoughts." She turned toward Derek. "Would you like to go first?"

Derek leaned back and sipped from a cup of coffee. "I'd like to hear what Tendo has in mind, then I'll pitch in afterward."

Vanya looked at Tendo. "Okay. Are you ready to go?"

"Yes." He turned his planner a few pages back to the notes he'd made earlier. "We need to give information to our potential customers from the time they're making interested inquiries and through their decision-making process until they finally become homeowners. Our first videos should be about educating potential homeowners. I've done a good deal of research to find out the top questions that are on these people's minds, and our videos need to answer these questions. The St. Mary Heath development is going to be targeted at a demographic that's aged over-fifty-five. We can deal with topics such as downsizing for empty-nesters, moving tips, and what the area has to offer for active retirees."

Vanya jotted notes as Tendo spoke. When he was done, she said, "That's a good start. Anything more to add, Derek? What could we reasonably take on and have ready within twelve weeks?"

Unlike Vanya, Derek had not made any notes while Tendo outlined his ideas. Derek said, "That's a solid meat-and-potatoes approach. However, I was thinking that within this three-month time frame, we need to hit hard on branding and company image. What makes Tymbrian Homes stand out among all the others? Quality, luxury, exclusivity. People are interested in the Klassen dream. That needs to be front and center. Tell your father's story and let people aspire to getting a piece of this lifestyle. We need to sell that dream, sell that aspiration."

Tendo stared at Derek. What sort of marketing background did this guy have? Did he have any clue about anything beyond yachts and llamas? But Vanya was nodding and writing things down in her notebook.

Tendo said, "I agree that we need to allow space to tell the company's story, and the overall Tymbrian Homes brand could go for an aspirational feel. But our aim is to give useful information first. We want to establish ourselves as the place potential customers go to when they want their questions answered, and provide immediate solutions that they can act on. It's not just about vague dreams, but actionable information, a number they can call, an expert they can talk to right now."

"Hmm," Derek said. He leaned back in his chair and laced his fingers behind his head. "Have a look at what Tymbrian Homes' main competitors are doing. I think you'll find that my ideas will fit in as well stand out. The difference between us and them is the Karl Klassen story."

Tendo's jaw tightened. "I have studied our competitors' marketing material in depth. With high-quality content packed with useful information, we could be thought leaders that convert traffic into sales. It's a proven strategy that has worked not just in our small pilot project here, but in several other industries."

Derek shrugged. "You're the marketing guru here, I suppose. All I know is how film moves people."

Tendo marveled at how Derek managed to pack a dismissive attitude into a seeming compliment.

Vanya looked back and forth between the two men. She finally spoke. "I can see both your points, and eventually I hope our video content will include both those aspects. But we have only three months left until the groundbreaking day. We have to pick one focus with the limited time we have."

She tapped her pen against her lips, and for a moment Tendo was distracted by their perfect shape and round contours. He blinked the thought away and focused on the question at hand. "The whole point of being a brand publisher is giving useful information to our customers."

"A brand publisher?" Derek said. "Isn't the operative word there *brand*?" He raised a dark eyebrow and let the question hang in the air.

Vanya stared at her planner, then looked first at Derek, then at Tendo. "I really like your idea, Tendo. But I think we'll go with Derek's plan first. After the groundbreaking ceremony is over, we'll continue creating the type of information-focused video content you want. I'm not dropping the idea completely, and you may go ahead with that angle on our blog and social media. But I feel Derek's ideas will have a stronger impact on video."

She turned to a fresh page in her diary. "Thanks, Tendo. You can get on with the rest of your work while Derek and I will get a bit more granular about his approach."

Tendo stood up, shaking his head. This is really what they wanted to do? Tymbrian Homes sold custom-built luxury homes that people bought at the blueprint level. Potential customers needed solid answers to practical questions as they prepared to spend a huge chunk of money. And Vanya thought it would be a good idea to show these people videos glorifying the company's founder? Well, it was the Klassens' funeral. All he did was work here. He headed back to his office.

Vanya watched Tendo leave. Had she made the right decision? What Tendo said had made a lot of sense until Derek started to speak. Derek did have a good point about Tymbrian Homes' competitors. She'd looked at their marketing materials and they were all very slick and style-focused, like ads for high-end vehicles. Style rather than substance. Was it a mistake to go in that direction?

Suddenly she wasn't sure anymore, and wished she could go through Tendo's ideas one more time. But Derek was talking about storyboards and she needed to pay attention to what he was saying. She quelled her doubts. The decision was made, and she needed to own it, double down, and move ahead.

After several minutes of discussion, Derek glanced at his watch, then turned his dimples on. "By the way, I've got an invitation to the grand opening of that new restaurant everyone's been buzzing about, Escam Elit. It'll be on Friday night. Would you care to join me? I can update you on any ideas I've thought up for the video project."

Vanya stared at his face and hesitated. Go out for dinner with Derek? He made it sound casual, but it was a meal out at one of the most hotly-anticipated new restaurants. She'd known him for years and his parents were close to hers, but she'd never spent much time alone with him. Despite her old schoolgirl crush, she'd known he was way out of her league. His name had been linked to a number of gorgeous young socialites and heiresses. Vanya was on the same social footing with them, but she was not the sort of bubbly arm candy Derek seemed to prefer. And yet it sounded like he was asking her on a date.

Her heart fluttered as she looked at his dark blue eyes. "Um, okay."

Within ten minutes of her dinner date, Vanya knew that coming out with Derek was a mistake. Escam Elit turned out to be a wine bar that also served food. While she liked the ambience of the cellar location with its high vaulted ceilings, rustic décor, and soft lighting, Derek sat a little too close and she had to remove his hand from her knee more than once.

After she turned down several suggestions of wine, he said, "Come on, Vanya. This is a wine bar. Won't you try one? How about a nice prosecco?"

Vanya struggled to keep the irritation out of her voice. How many times did she have to say no? "I'll be fine with soda water or fruit juice if they have it."

He tilted his head and stared at her for a moment, then shrugged. "Okay. Excuse me!" He signaled a waiter and the two of them had a whispered consultation while Vanya looked around her, admiring the exposed brick on the walls. It would have been a romantic place to enjoy a meal, given the right person.

The waiter hurried off, and Derek turned back to Vanya. "How are you enjoying the new job?"

"I'm settling in. Things are moving along fine."

"What's up with this Tandoori fellow? Is that his name? Tinder? Tender?"

"Tendo," Vanya said. "What do you mean?"

"I just wondered. He seems pretty sure of himself."

Vanya frowned. "He's good at what he does."

"Hmm." Derek rested his elbows on the table and leaned toward Vanya. "You want to be careful. I know his type. Chip on his shoulder the size of an anvil. They feel the world owes them a favor."

Vanya squirmed in her seat. She had her reservations about Tendo, but she didn't like the tone of Derek's comments. Her unease with her deputy was because she wasn't sure she measured up to his high standards. She wanted to shut this line of conversation down immediately. "He may not be the most mellow or agreeable person, but he's been nothing but professional."

Derek looked as though he wanted to say more, but the waiter came by with a tray bearing two drinks: a glass of wine and what appeared to be juice, garnished with a straw and thick slices of orange. He placed both glasses on the table with a flourish, then bustled away.

Derek picked up the wine glass and held it aloft. "Cheers."

Vanya sipped her drink. It was a delicious blend of tropical fruit juice. She could taste pineapple, passion fruit, and—she swallowed and then coughed as a trail of heat seared its way down her throat. She put the glass down and glared at Derek. "What's in this? I told you I don't drink alcohol."

Derek smirked. "You said you'd never developed a taste for it. I thought if you had a bit of rum punch it would teach you how delicious a little tipple can be. Plus, we could loosen up a little. Something tells me you could be quite a bit of fun if you let your hair down. Go on.

Try some." He winked at her and stroked her arm.

Vanya shuddered and pulled away from his touch. She was seeing him in a completely new light. What she had once thought of as his roguish charm now looked and felt more like sinister manipulation. The last vestiges of her schoolgirl crush shriveled and died, and she couldn't wait to get away. She picked up her purse. "I have to go."

His eyes widened. "I thought we were going to have dinner."

"No, thank you. I'll see you next week."

She stood up and hurried out, sensing his gaze on her.

Chapter Ten

VER THE next few weeks, Tendo focused on bringing the new hires on board and setting them to work on his brutal content schedule. He had to admit that, despite his objections, Pamela had been a great choice as lead copywriter.

She was a tireless ball of energy and absorbed whatever tasks he threw at her. She worked like a machine, writing with speed and flair. And Vanya had been right about Pamela's creativity. She came up with a few oddball suggestions, but most of her ideas were excellent, quirky, and fun. The Tymbrian Homes blog was growing quickly, and traffic had never been higher.

Pamela came up to Tendo's desk, pen and notebook in hand, clearly bursting to tell him something. She changed her hair color every few days and this week, her shaggy bob was peacock blue. "Hey, guess what?"

He smiled. "What?"

"Ever heard of Julia Rae?"

Tendo dredged his memory but came up empty. "No. Who's she?"

"Julia Rae? The Rae family?" Tendo shook his head and Pamela laughed. "Clearly you're not a fan of YouTube mummy vlogs."

She pulled up a chair and sat in front of his desk. "She's got a popular channel on YouTube. I'm talking *huge*. Ten million subscribers, about five hundred videos, each one with an average of fifteen million views. Anyway, I heard on the grapevine—

and don't ask me how I know, because if I tell you I'll need to kill you—that she is about to close on a Tymbrian Homes house. What do you think about asking her to be a brand ambassador for us and make a series on her vlog about buying and moving into her new Tymbrian home?"

Tendo stared at Pamela for a long moment, then laughed. "You're a genius. I don't know how you do it. That would be a fantastic idea if— and it's a huge if—all the moving pieces fall into place."

Pamela poised her pen over her notebook. "What are these pieces? Let's see how they move and how we can get them to fall into place."

Tendo smiled again. He loved this girl's get up and go attitude. "We'd need to vet this lady thoroughly. Or as thoroughly as we can, I mean. No skeletons lurking in her closet. Do a deep dive into her social media accounts to make sure she didn't say something iffy on Twitter ten years ago. Find out exactly what the company's policy on brand ambassadors is. I think they'd be okay in principle, but we need to confirm it. I'm not entirely sure about confidentiality, but we have to crosscheck whether she is, in fact, in the process of buying a Tymbrian home. That should probably be the first thing we check. And after we've done all that, we'd need to see whether she'd be interested in vlogging the process for us."

Pamela looked up from the notes she was taking. "Oh, she'll be interested. She's the product placement queen. I think everything down to her dinner plates gets some sort of corporate sponsorship."

Tendo raised his eyebrows. "Is that so? I'm not sure whether that's a good thing or a bad thing."

"I'm an optimist. I'm going to say it's a good thing."

"Perhaps. But we've got a long way to go before we even get to the point where we can approach her. And, of course, we'll need to run it by Vanya."

Pamela chewed the end of her pen. "But can we start the preliminary process? Finding out the company's brand ambassador policy and whether Julia is actually closing on a Tymbrian Home?"

"Yes, let's go ahead with that. I'll check on the company policy on brand ambassadors and whether Julia's a customer, and you can begin digging into her social media accounts."

Pamela grinned. "Ooh, social media snooping. And you'll actually pay me for this?"

Tendo chuckled as Pamela went back to her desk. He headed toward Vanya's office. Pamela's idea had huge potential, but he ought to run it by Vanya to see what she thought.

He got to the doorway of her office and saw her standing facing the window, her back toward him, cell phone pressed on her ear. Her voice sounded strained as she tried several times to get a word in edgewise with the person she was speaking to. "I— yes, but... I get it, Derek. But—"

Finally, after listening for a long while she said, "I understand what you're saying, but here's the thing. It's been two weeks since we were supposed to have had the first video ready, but I haven't even seen a rough edit."

She listened for a moment, then threw up a hand in a gesture of frustration. "You do know that we've got only six weeks left until the groundbreaking celebration, right? And we'll need a video series to launch by then." She rubbed the back of her neck and leaned forward, her fore-head resting on the windowpane.

Tendo shuffled his feet and Vanya turned around, her body straightening up as she saw him in the doorway. She spoke into the phone again. "Listen, I have to go, but please remember time is running out. And when will I see that rough edit?" She listened some more then sighed, clearly not happy with the answer she got. "Right, then. Bye."

Vanya looked up at Tendo, turning the phone around in her hands. "What's going on?"

"I wanted to run something by you quickly. It's an idea Pamela came up with, and I think it's a good one."

She walked forward, brushing past him briefly as she made her way back to her desk. He was distracted by the scent of her perfume, something light and floral he couldn't identify. He leaned forward involuntarily, straining to catch another breath of it. She settled into her chair and motioned for him to sit down. "Let's hear it."

He sat on the edge of the armchair. "There's a mummy vlogger with a huge YouTube following and Pamela's heard that she's buying a house from Tymbrian Homes. Pamela thinks we might be able to get her to vlog about the whole experience and be a brand ambassador."

Vanya tilted her head backward and rubbed the side of her neck with one hand as Tendo spoke. She looked tired. "Is she someone we'd want to be associated with?"

"Pamela's looking more closely into that. Do we have a policy on brand ambassadors?"

Vanya frowned. "I'm not sure. Juan Martinez, that pro-golfer who won the Masters a couple of years ago, has done some promotional events for our golfing facilities. That's the closest thing I can think of off the top of my head. I'll have to ask Suzy." She picked up a pen and looked up at Tendo. "It sounds like a good idea, by the way."

"That's what I thought. If it does pan out, we'd need to move quickly." He paused while Vanya made a note in her planner. "How's Derek's video series coming along?"

She shot him a quick glance, her cheeks coloring. "Did you hear me talking on the phone? It's a bit behind schedule, but he expects things to move forward a lot more quickly from now on."

Not the impression I got, Tendo thought. Aloud, he said, "There's something else I wanted to ask you about. The copywriters are having a hard time pinning down people who are supposed to give us more information for our blog."

"Which people are these?"

"Pamela needs to get ahold of someone from the architecture

department to talk about our house designs, and Melissa hasn't had much luck finding someone who can tell her about landscaping and mortgage options."

Vanya scribbled down some notes in her planner. "And this is for the blog, you said?"

"Yes. They need to interview in-house experts so we can get some good quotes to make our articles sound more authoritative."

"I'll talk to their department heads and ask them to make it a priority." She looked up at him. "I like how the blog is taking shape."

"It's coming along well." He paused and added, "You made a very good call about hiring Pamela, by the way. You were right on the money about her."

She smiled, and it eased some of the lines of tension on her face. "Thanks. I had a good feeling about her." She took a breath. He thought she wanted to say something more, but instead she closed her mouth and reached for her phone. "I'll try to get things moving with your subject matter experts."

He understood the meeting was over and stood up to leave.

Tendo didn't know what Vanya said to the department heads, but it had an immediate effect. Pamela and Melissa both got emails from the people they'd been trying to chase down for weeks, and they headed out of the office to do the interviews they needed for their blog posts.

Vanya also sent Tendo an email telling him that the company did have a brand ambassador policy, and she quoted and linked to the relevant sections of the marketing plan.

She copied Tendo in on an email exchange with the sales department, which confirmed that Julia Rae was in the late stages of purchasing a property from Tymbrian Homes. It was a green light to carry on with vetting the mommy vlogger.

He had to hand it to Vanya: she could get things moving. All he had to do was mention a bureaucratic or logistical roadblock and she found a way around or through it. It was a refreshing change from working with Suzy, whose mission seemed to be to obstruct and demoralize rather than help her team.

Everything was chugging along nicely, apart from the big video project. As far as he was aware, Derek had not yet completed a single video of the series that was supposed to be the key component of their promotion. Well, Vanya had not thought it fit to keep him in the loop about what was going on there, so it wasn't his problem.

Chapter Eleven

VANYA STARED at the tablet screen in front of her, unable to believe what she'd seen. She blinked for several moments, then looked at Derek. He sat opposite her, slouched in an armchair, one eyebrow quirked to match the crooked smirk on his face.

"Well?" he asked. "What do you think?"

She gestured at the screen and shook her head. This is what you got when you didn't check on what your videographer was up to. "I don't know what to say."

His smile widened. "It's good, isn't it?"

"It's an interesting take on my father." The ten-minute black and white video was slick and well-produced, showing clips of Karl Klassen striding around with purpose across marble-floored lobbies, dominating on the tennis court, steering a luxury yacht with the wind in his handsome face and well-coiffed iron gray hair.

Excerpts of *Invictus*, Karl's favorite poem, flashed across the screen, intercut with the images of her father. Vanya knew that Karl would probably like it, but this was nowhere near what she had imagined.

She groped for the words to use. "It's not a bad film, but it says nothing about Tymbrian Homes. This is supposed to be the central piece in our marketing for people who want to buy homes, but there's nothing there that tells homeowners anything about doing business with us. It's impossible to use."

Derek's eyebrows lowered. "My brief was to produce a piece that brings across the Karl Klassen lifestyle, the dream that your customers are aspiring to reach. That film distills the essence of that dream, that spirit, and captures your father's brand. This is what I was asked to do."

"Yes, but you were supposed to do it in a way that supports our sales team when they're trying to actually sell our off-plan homes." Vanya closed her eyes for a moment and massaged her temples. "What else have you got? You were producing a series, right?"

Derek glowered. "We've got five, three, and one-minute versions of the same film. I stuck to the brief you gave me. This is top quality material, and your father approves of it."

"He's already seen it?" Vanya couldn't imagine that her father could have okayed this. Maybe he liked it as a self-promotional tool, but surely he could see it was outside the purpose of what her team needed.

"Of course he's seen it," Derek said, reaching out and taking his tablet back. "He thinks it's great."

"I'm sure we can use it in some way, but not for the current campaign we have in mind. Can we have a new discussion just to clarify exactly what message we're hoping this video series will put across?"

Derek sighed heavily. "Fine."

He was acting more like a sulky teenager than a grown man with a job to deliver. Ignoring his heavy sighing, Vanya said, "Shall we discuss it now? I can pull in a couple of people and we could put our heads together and figure out a way forward."

Derek looked at his watch. "Now's actually not a great time. I've got a lunch appointment. Could we meet later in the afternoon?"

"Two o'clock?"

"Make it three." He stood up and headed for the door. "See you then."

He walked out, and Vanya groaned aloud. What a nightmare this was. The niggling alarm bell she'd had in the back of her mind had now blossomed into a full-blown siren.

Derek had finally shown her what he'd been working on for the past eight weeks, and it was not going to be usable.

And now, there were only four weeks until the groundbreaking ceremony.

She remembered Tendo's words about the direction their video series should take and how she'd decided to trust Derek's judgment instead.

She sat for a moment, shoulders sagging, chewing the end of one thumb. The rest of their content marketing was making excellent progress. Under Tendo's direction, the copywriting and social media team had created thriving channels on Pinterest, Twitter, Instagram, and Facebook. Tendo had shared the latest numbers in their standup meeting that morning, and their traffic was higher than their most optimistic projections. If only they had the video content to go with all of it.

Her stomach growled, a reminder that breakfast had been hours ago. The cafeteria would just be opening now. She could grab a quick bite as soon as she'd sent an email to her team asking them to meet with her and Derek later that afternoon. When she'd sent the email, she headed to the cafeteria, the smells inviting her in. Herb-roasted chicken was the main entree today, with ratatouille as the vegetarian alternative.

She went for the ratatouille and oven-roasted root vegetables and looked around her for a table. There weren't many people in the cafeteria yet, but her eyes went immediately to a group close to the windows.

Tendo was sitting there, along with Pamela, copywriter Melissa, and Omar, the social media specialist who rounded out their team. Vanya walked toward them slowly. Although she didn't want company, it would look odd if she sat alone in the corner.

Pamela, sporting a plume of hair the color of pink cotton candy, was in the middle of a story that had the rest of the group in stitches. But as soon as Vanya drew closer, their eyes flew toward her and the laughter fell silent, their expressions toning down into polite smiles. She hesitated, feeling like she'd just intruded on their fun. She was about to nod and move past when Tendo gestured with a hand.

"Please join us." He made room next to him on the bench, and as Vanya sat down he said, "Pamela was just telling us about her date from hell. Go on, Pam."

Pamela took up her story, and everyone was soon laughing again. Vanya relaxed while she ate her lunch and let the words wash around her. When Pamela ended her anecdote, she turned to Vanya. "What about you? Any nightmare date stories?"

Vanya dabbed at her lips with a napkin. She stifled a shudder as she remembered her evening out with Derek. There was no way she would share that disaster. Smiling, she decided to match Pamela's light tone. "There was the time my mother set me up with her dentist's son."

Pamela's eyes went round. "No way! Whose mother fixes dates for them?"

Tendo held up a hand, setting off fresh peals of laughter around the table. "Hey, don't knock it," he said. "There's something to be said for the old ways."

Omar chuckled. "Then why are you still single?"

"Because sometimes the execution fails, even when the principle is sound. I got so busy at work that I completely forgot my mum had set up a blind date for me. I stood the girl up and she refused to meet me again."

Everyone laughed, and Tendo turned to Vanya. "I'd like to hear about this dentist's son."

She quirked an eyebrow. "Are you sure you want to hear this while you're eating?"

"Ooh, sounds like a good one. Go on," Pamela said.

"He took me on his speedboat, and I was seasick the whole time." As everyone groaned, she added, "And he didn't have sick bags."

Pamela slapped her cutlery onto her plate. "That's it. Lunch is over."

Vanya laughed. "I gave you fair warning!"

"Yeah, you did."

The banter continued a while longer until Vanya noticed how full the cafeteria was getting. She glanced at her watch. "I'd better get back to work. I sent all of you an email just before I came down about a meeting we're having with our videographer at three o'clock." She caught Tendo's expression as she spoke. His smile faded as though she'd thrown a damp blanket over the previously warm and bubbly group.

"What's it about?" Tendo asked.

"We need a change of direction with our video series," Vanya said.

She stood and looked at all their faces. She added, "I hope you're able to make it. I could use your input." She didn't mean to sound as needy as she did, but Melissa and Pamela smiled warmly at her.

She took her food tray to the collection rack, praying silently that her team would be able to figure out a way to get something usable out of Derek's footage.

Chapter Twelve

As THEY left the cafeteria, Tendo let the others go up to the office ahead of him. He needed to swing by the marketing department to clarify a couple of points about the company's brand ambassador policy. The plan to recruit the mommy vlogger to promote Tymbrian Homes was gathering steam, barring a few small issues that needed ironing out.

Lunch had been a lot of fun today. He and his team often ate together, but it was the first time Vanya had joined them. It had been nice to know she could let her hair down and join in the friendly banter. She had a down-to-earth human side. And by the sound of it, she'd had dating trouble, too. He wondered why an attractive woman like her was still single.

He'd thought that there might have been something brewing between her and Derek when the videographer had first come on board. But since then, she'd treated Derek with nothing more than a brisk politeness. In any case, that was completely irrelevant. Her love life was none of his business.

When Tendo got back to the office, everyone was gathered around Omar's computer. As soon as he stepped inside, the huddle broke up and Pamela and Melissa began moving back toward their desks, eyes averted from his. His curiosity was piqued. "Okay, guys. What have you been looking at?" Three pairs of eyes turned toward him and slid away again. He walked up to Omar's desk and spoke to the younger man. "What is it? Hope you haven't been surfing material you shouldn't be looking at."

Color flooded Omar's face and he stammered, "No! It's not anything like that." He turned his gaze toward Pamela, his eyes pleading.

Pamela came back and faced Tendo. "It's just something on YouTube the guys from marketing sent us. Show him, Omar."

Omar clicked his screen, and a video began to play. It was footage of what appeared to be a public event, a dinner of some kind. Vanya stood in front of a lectern, grabbing its edges with white-knuckled hands. She faced an audience, and there was a strained silence broken only as a murmur rippled through the crowd. Vanya's face crumpled and she began to sob before fleeing from the lectern. A loud buzz of talk began, and the camera followed Vanya as she stumbled between the dinner tables and out of the room.

"What is this?" Tendo asked. He grabbed the mouse from Omar and scrolled down. The video had been uploaded just a couple of weeks ago. The first viewer comment caught his eye: a crude joke about Vanya. The one below wasn't much better. "What is this?" he asked again.

Pamela answered, "Looks like a big gala event. The caption says it happened about three or four months ago."

Tendo read the video description and did a quick mental calculation. This would have been recorded shortly before Vanya started working at Tymbrian Homes. Is this why she'd left her previous job?

He closed the browser window and looked around at his team members. "Let's leave that right there. I'm sure none of us would like our worst moment captured on video and uploaded to YouTube."

Omar, Pamela, and Melissa voiced their assent and got back to their desks. Tendo sat in front of his own computer, wondering what he'd been looking at. He was tempted to do a Google search and find out more, but he already felt as though he had pried open a secret door and stared at something private. Whatever Vanya had been going through at that moment, he hoped she was past it. Nice of whoever that was to put it on YouTube, though.

Although he made his living by the Internet, sometimes he hated it with a passion.

Chapter Thirteen

A FEW DAYS later, Vanya stared at her phone screen, praying the message she was reading was a prank. It was from Derek. ***Had to take a trip abroad to handle an unexpected family situation. Sorry about short notice. See you when I get back.***

She dropped the phone onto her desk and paced around the room, flexing and unflexing her hands. Her mother had been talking last night about the Coleman-Bainses going to their Swiss chalet. Vanya had strong suspicions that Derek's trip was less of a family emergency and more of a skiing holiday. Three weeks from the launch of the video series he was producing, a series which had needed to be started from scratch last week, and he had gone to frolic on the Alpine slopes.

How would she fix this? She stopped her pacing. She needed to ask Tendo for help and admit that the videographer she'd brought onto the team had dropped the ball. Would he take advantage of this? Suzy had warned her about Tendo's ambition. Just last week, she'd said, "You can't ever show a guy like that weakness. He's after your job and he'll do everything he can to under-mine you."

Maybe Suzy was right and Tendo might see this situation as leverage with which to pull himself higher at Vanya's expense. She couldn't af-ford to think about that now, though. Right now, she needed to figure out how to get some high-quality video content produced in three weeks, and she could not do that without Tendo's help.

She went down the hallway to the office Tendo shared with the rest of the content marketing team. Thank God Tendo was there. She went up to his desk. "Do you have a moment? I need to talk to you in my office."

He looked up at her. "Sure. I'll finish this up and see you in five minutes."

She went back to her office, her heart racing, trying to focus her thoughts. Tendo came in. Without any preamble she said, "We're up the creek. I just heard from Derek. He's gone on a trip with no word about when he'll be back.

Tendo stared at her. "Derek's gone? So, where does that leave the material he was working on? Will he be able to turn it over in time?"

Vanya shook her head. "I don't think so."

"Did he leave a contact number for somebody from his team who could tell us whether they have anything we can use?"

Vanya cringed inside. She ought to have thought of that. She was so agitated over Derek's message that her mind wasn't working right. She went to her desk and clicked her computer on. "I'll see if there's anyone I can talk to."

Tendo moved over to the sofa and pulled out his phone while Vanya clicked through her email correspondence with Derek. After a couple of minutes, she said, "Here's a number I can use."

A female voice answered after a couple of rings. "Coleman-Baines Videography. How can I help you?"

"Hi. My name is Vanya Klassen from Tymbrian Homes. Derek has been working on a project with us. I understand he's away, but I wondered whether there's anyone else who can update me on the status of my project."

"Hold on a minute, please."

Vanya drummed her fingers on her desk as she waited. At least they had nice hold music. Mozart's Symphony in G Minor had always been a favorite.

The woman came back on the line. "Hello. Did you say your name was Klassen? I've spoken to our project manager and he tells me that Mr. Coleman-Baines was personally overseeing your project. He's the only one who can give you an accurate update about where the work stands. I'm very sorry, but I'm sure that Mr. Coleman-Baines will be in touch as soon as he can. It was an unfortunate family situation."

I'll bet, Vanya thought. He'll be in touch as soon as whatever party he's gone to breaks up. But there was nothing more to be gained from this conversation. "Thanks for your help," she said, ending the call. She looked up at Tendo. "They can't tell us anything. Derek was overseeing the project and we won't know what's going on until he can tell us."

Tendo held up his phone. "This might be a long shot, but there's a videographer I've worked with in the past. She's really good and might be able to help us out. I know she's super fast."

Vanya looked up at him, her heart beginning to thud. "A videographer? What kind of work can she do?"

"I've worked with her to do corporate videos in the past, and I know she's done documentaries and interviews. Shall I give her a call?"

Vanya nodded. "Please! Yes. What's her name?"

"Eden Tracy. I'll just call her." Tendo punched his phone and waited for a moment. "Hey, Eden. Yes, it's been ages! Listen, I need a huge favor. Are you by any chance able to drop everything and take on a new project?"

Vanya watched Tendo's face as he spoke, holding her breath as she waited for an answer.

Tendo spoke again. "Really? That's awesome! Do you think you could come to… hang on a minute." He put his hand over his phone and looked at Vanya. "Shall we try to talk with her today?"

When Vanya nodded, he spoke into the phone again. "Our offices are at Canary Wharf, and we'd need you to clear at least a month off your schedule. Three weeks at the very least. I'll text you our address. It would be awesome if you could come over as soon as you can. Tymbrian Homes. Just ask for me. See you soon."

He hung up and looked up at Vanya. "She's on her way."

An hour and a half later, Vanya sat in the conference room with Tendo, the rest of her team, and the person she hoped could dig them out of the pit Derek had created. Eden, her long dark hair swept away from her face in a smooth ponytail, looked like she'd be better suited striking a pose in front of the camera rather than behind it as a videographer.

But Vanya's confidence grew as the meeting carried on. Eden showed a keen and quick mind, speedily grasping what the Tymbrian Homes team wanted her to do.

After listening to Vanya and Tendo speak and asking several questions, Eden tapped her pen against her teeth and sat in silence for a moment. "I think we can do this, but it will be tight. If you can figure out exactly how many films you want me to make and what you want the content to be, it would give me a better handle on how much work would be involved. But from what you've said so far, it sounds fairly straightforward. We're not trying to win a film award, right? You just want simple informational videos."

Vanya nodded vigorously. "Absolutely." She looked around at her team. "We don't have any time to waste. Let's decide right now the sorts of videos we want to make so that Eden can start getting prepared."

She turned to Tendo. "We'll go with your original proposal for this project. Any ideas we can throw together within three weeks?"

He smiled. "As a matter of fact, there are. The first thing we could do is an FAQ in video form. It would be a series of short videos, each covering the biggest questions our sales team gets when they talk to potential customers. I'm thinking short interviews with some of the sales, architecture, or mortgage teams, or anyone else with relevant knowledge. They could be done fairly quickly." He turned to Eden. "Does that make sense?"

Eden nodded. "Totally."

Pamela chimed in. "Another thing I've heard can be really helpful is to have a short video on any content that includes a sign-up form. Wherever we're asking people to give us their contact details, we can have a video that tells them what the form is for and what will happen after they sign up. I've heard these can boost conversions in a massive way. If we don't want to have more talking heads, perhaps we could make it an animated video?"

Eden looked up from the notes she was scribbling. "Great idea. I can think of a couple of possible treatments and get back to you."

"And then we've also got our testimonial videos," Pamela said. "Happy customers who can give us short remarks about how pleased they are to be living in a Tymbrian Home."

Eden glanced at Vanya. "These are great ideas, but you said we have only three weeks. Which of these video types is most important for you to publish first?"

Vanya looked at Tendo. "What do you think? FAQs?"

Tendo nodded. "Yes, we need to prioritize the FAQ videos. After that, I'd say the ones that go with sign-up pages. These would probably have the biggest impact on turning curious browsers into buying customers. The video testimonials are a great idea, but given the time crunch we're in, I doubt we could get them done before the launch."

Vanya said, "I agree, especially since we might need more than three weeks to get customers to agree to endorse us on camera."

They talked a bit more, then Eden closed her notebook. "This is a good amount to get started with. I need to run a few numbers past my partner. We'll come back to you with a proposal by the end of the day. I'll make a quick call now so he can get started."

Vanya smiled. She felt a burden lifting from her shoulders. "Sounds great."

Eden pulled out her phone and moved a few steps toward the window to make her call.

Tendo stood and glanced around at the other members of the team. "Let's get back to work, people. Pamela and Melissa, it would be awesome if you could grab that FAQ list from our blog and figure out who we'll ask to give the answers on screen."

As the team members began to leave, Vanya touched Tendo's arm. "Hang on a minute."

He turned around to look at her. The simple words of thanks she'd planned to say suddenly seemed inadequate. This morning her plans had lain in tatters. But thanks to Tendo's stepping up and pulling in the people she needed, they still had a shot at making their deadline. "I just..." Her throat ached, making it hard to speak. She swallowed hard. "Thank you."

He looked at her in silence for a moment, a smile warming up his eyes. "No thanks needed. We're in this together, right?"

She smiled back. For the first time, she felt as though they were.

Chapter Fourteen

THE VIDEO came to an end and Tendo rubbed his eyes. They were gritty with fatigue, but before he went home, he wanted to check this last batch of videos Eden had sent through. Her team had filmed Tymbrian Homes staff members answering frequently asked questions.

The footage was taken in one of the show homes and the speakers came across as relaxed, articulate, and knowledgeable. He typed up an email asking the website manager to upload them tomorrow.

It was all hands on deck now, the way it had been since Derek's disappearing act. Tendo wasn't sure what the man was doing. But since Vanya hadn't mentioned him and he hadn't shown up around the office, Tendo assumed the launch was going forward with Eden's videos, and they would continue with the original video content strategy he'd wanted all along.

He finished writing his email and sent it off, then shut his computer down. His mother was not going to be happy that he'd worked late again, but she understood this was crunch time for this project. She had started making noises about wanting to move into a place of her own, but he'd been adamant that she wasn't going back to the Wood Green Estate.

Since Enid had documented the harassment she'd suffered in her home, the housing association had agreed that she could transfer to another house on a different estate, but she had to go on the waiting list until a suitable property became available. There was no guarantee when that would be. Enid had flat out refused to let Tendo pay for her to rent from a private landlord, insisting her stay with him would only be temporary.

"What about when you meet a nice girl and want her to visit you at home? You can't have your mother hanging around," Enid had said.

"I don't think that will be a problem, Mum," Tendo had said.

It was nice having her around, and he was getting used to finding a warm meal waiting for him at home.

He picked up his jacket and stepped out into the hallway, running straight into somebody who was walking past his door. "Whoa," he said, holding out his hands to steady her. It was Vanya.

She straightened up and brushed a strand of blond hair off her cheek. "Sorry. I normally look where I'm going when I walk."

"No, it's my fault. You okay?" He drew his hands back. "I didn't know anyone else was here."

"I was looking at Eden's videos. She's done a tremendous job." She fiddled with the strap of her handbag, and looked back up at him. "I think we might actually pull this off. Thanks for recommending Eden."

He smiled. "I'm glad she's making me look good. I knew she was excellent at her job, but she's hit it out of the park."

Vanya took a step down the hallway and he walked alongside her, glancing at her out of the corner of his eye. Was she going to the train station? There were occasionally some rough types hanging around at this time of the night. He wasn't worried for himself using public transit, but with her clearly expensive clothes and handbag and her high-heeled shoes, she could all too easily attract the wrong kind of attention traveling late and on her own.

He cleared his throat. "Are you going to take the train home? I'm on my way to the station and can walk you there."

Her eyes widened, then her features relaxed into a smile. "No, but thank you. I've arranged a ride home."

Of course, he thought, giving himself a mental shake. Karl Klassen's daughter was probably using Daddy's chauffeur. She didn't need the Tendos of this world to worry about how she was getting home. It was none of his business, anyway.

He nodded. "See you tomorrow."

"Good night."

Chapter Fifteen

ANYA STOOD toward the back of the crowd, watching as her father lined up alongside a collection of investors and dignitaries from the county council. Each of them wore hardhats and grasped ceremonial shovels as they smiled for the cameras.

The groundbreaking ceremony was going well. All around the stage were banners with Tymbrian Homes' distinctive branding displaying the website address and social media handles that would take people to the company's new content marketing campaign.

Eden's team had been busy today filming the ceremony and speeches and interviewing dignitaries and attendees. They would take the footage back and edit it down into news-style pieces which would be uploaded onto the Tymbrian Homes website later this evening once Vanya had given her final approval.

She looked across the crowd where Tendo stood talking to somebody from the videography team. She took a deep breath and slowly let it out. They had actually pulled it off. The video series had gone live yesterday, along with Omar's internet and social media advertising campaign, and the clicks were rolling in. The sales department was thrilled with the uptick in leads they were getting. Derek was maintaining radio silence and she didn't care if she never heard from him again. Although it would feel wonderful to terminate his contract. She'd been so busy that she hadn't had time to get that process going.

Eden came up, equipment bag slung over her shoulder. "We're about done here, so we'll go back and process what we've got. Pamela's emailing us a script for the graphics and voiceovers, and we'll send you a three-minute news piece in three or four hours. We'll also get the dignitaries' interviews done in separate clips. Those will be ready later on tonight."

Vanya smiled. "That's perfect. Then we can get that all uploaded onto the website." For all of Derek's bragging about showing at the Cannes Film Festival, she couldn't imagine his team being as efficient as Eden's. As Eden turned to go, Vanya said, "Thanks so much. This will wrap up our current contract, but I think it's safe to say you'll hear back from us very soon about more work. Please keep your calendar clear."

Eden returned her smile. "Thank you. It's been a pleasure. Speak to you soon." She walked away and Vanya stood for a moment watching everyone mingle.

"You look pleased."

She whirled around to see Tendo standing next to her. "That's because I am. I still can't believe this all came off."

"We've got a great team," he said.

"We do. That reminds me: I wanted to tell Melissa and Pamela they can go straight home after this. They've done a tremendous job."

She reached into her bag for her phone, but Tendo said, "I already did. I told Pamela I'll put together the writeup and send the videographers the info they need. On which note, I need to get back to the office."

"I'll come too," Vanya said. "I brought my own car today, so I could give you a ride if you need it."

His white teeth flashed in a smile. "Perfect. That'll save me from taking the train back. I can do the write-up while we're on the road and send it off as soon as we're back in London."

They were edging their way around a group of guests when Vanya heard her father's deep gravelly voice. "Vanya. A moment, please." Karl detached himself from the people he'd been talking to and approached her, lips tilting in a smile. "Are you heading off?"

"Yes. We've got a few things to do back at the office."

Karl turned to look at Tendo, who stood a couple of feet behind Vanya. "There you are, Tendo. Excellent work, both of you. I got an update from the sales department and they're thoroughly pleased with the material you've given them to work with."

Tendo inclined his head. "Thank you, sir. Our team has worked very hard."

"I won't keep you. Go make us more sales."

He went back to his associates and Vanya and Tendo made their way to the parking area. Vanya tried to pick her way carefully, but her heels sank into the ground made soft by a steady drizzle in the morning.

They got to her car and she opened the door, stashing her bag while Tendo slid into the passenger seat and opened up his laptop.

Vanya said, "Could you give me those shoes over there? Just under your feet."

Tendo wriggled around, balancing his computer on his knees as he reached under his seat. He pulled up a pair of pink moccasins. "You mean these?"

She took them from him. "Thanks. They're my driving shoes." She sat down and replaced her pumps with the soft comfortable shoes, wriggling her toes in relief.

"I always wondered how women drive in those things," Tendo said, eyeing her pumps as she twisted her body to set her muddy pumps on the floor behind her.

"We don't. Or at least I don't. It's hard to have full control of the pedals when you're in high heels."

He clicked his seatbelt in place. "Thank you. That's one of life's great mysteries solved. I've always wondered."

Vanya smiled. "Glad to be of service."

She started up the engine and navigated the car onto the road. Tendo turned his attention to his laptop and they drove in silence as she took them through the feeder roads and eventually merged onto the M25.

Vanya stole a glance at him, catching a view of his profile as he worked. He'd pushed the seat far back to accommodate his tall frame and his fingers flew over the keyboard. He typed with few pauses, writing with the same efficiency and focus with which he approached everything he did.

She had decided a long time ago that Suzy had been completely wrong about Tendo. For reasons she didn't fully understand, Suzy had completely misrepresented him. While Tendo was self-assured, he wasn't conceited, as his former manager had claimed. He demanded a lot from his team, but pushed himself just as hard.

Perhaps he and Suzy had simply never hit it off. Since Vanya had known her back in school, Suzy had never had kind words to say about any boys who hadn't swooned at her feet. She saw herself as a femme fatale and inferred that if a guy didn't fall for her charms, there must be something strange about him.

Vanya was glad Tendo hadn't responded to Suzy's raw and blunt sex appeal. Suzy was not the kind to keep a romantic conquest secret and would have told Vanya if she'd had a fling with Tendo. Vanya's face warmed up. It wasn't any concern of hers who Tendo did or didn't fall for. She needed to distract herself from this train of thought.

"Do you mind if I turn on the radio for a bit?" she asked.

"No, it's fine. I'm nearly finished, anyway."

Her eyebrows flew up. "Really? That was quick."

"Pamela had already written up the meat of it. I only needed to include a few extra details."

"Awesome. Where did you learn to type like that?"

He looked at her and grinned. "My stepdad made me learn the summer before I went to university. I grumbled a bit at the time, but it was the best decision ever. It made my life a lot easier."

"I can imagine. Touch typing was an elective subject in my school, and I skipped it. I just hunt and peck. Was it hard to learn?"

"Not at all. I learned where the keys were within a couple of days, and after that it's just practice."

She drove quietly for a while longer, an easy listening track playing softly in the background.

As they got closer to central London, Vanya's hands tightened on the steering wheel. The increasingly congested traffic meant she needed to concentrate more on the road and less on the man beside her. She didn't often drive into the city, and the heavy traffic around her was a reminder why. She sometimes got a ride to work with Karl and his chauffeur, but more often came by public transit. Karl didn't often get to his desk before nine thirty, which was far too late for her.

They finally got to the tall gleaming buildings of Canary Wharf, and Vanya steered the car into a reserved spot in the parking garage underneath the Tymbrian Homes offices. She opened the back passenger door and reached for her pumps, then made a face. She'd forgotten how muddy they'd gotten. She dropped them back on the car floor and slung her bag over her shoulder. She'd have to keep her driving moccasins on, although they were a strange contrast to her belted Gucci shift dress.

Tendo was already out of the car, and he followed her as they headed for the elevator. "I'll mail this writeup straight over to Eden so they can finish the videos."

"Great stuff," Vanya said, as the doors slid open. They stepped inside and as the doors shut them in the enclosed space, she was keenly aware of Tendo's presence. When she was without her usual high heels, he towered over her. The silence stretched as the elevator moved up the floors. She spoke at the same time Tendo broke the silence. They both chuckled and she said, "Go ahead."

"I, um, was just going to suggest..." he hesitated for a moment. "It'll be a while until Eden's done and I'm pretty hungry. Would you like to grab a bite while we wait for the videos to come through?"

Warmth spread through Vanya. "Great idea. I didn't get much lunch with all the rushing around."

He smiled at her. "Cool."

Chapter Sixteen

THEY WENT to a small Italian restaurant that Tendo suggested. Vanya's eyes grew wide as the waiters brought their orders over. "You weren't lying when you said the pizzas are the size of a bicycle wheel." She stared at hers and wondered how she was going to get it all down.

Tendo grinned at her over his super-sized calzone. "The crust is almost paper thin, so it's not as massive as it looks."

She picked up a slice and closed her eyes as her teeth sank into the prosciutto and Parmesan. She didn't know whether it was because she was hungry, but she couldn't remember ever eating a pizza so delicious. Tendo's eyes were on her and she held up her hand and nodded while she finished her mouthful. "It's amazing," she said.

"Glad you like it." He held up his calzone "This is pretty awesome, too."

She finished her first piece and ate a second one. Her mother would have had several things to say if she'd seen Vanya putting away a pizza this size. In silent defiance, Vanya picked up another slice and ate it with relish. She looked around at the small restaurant with its cozy booths, distressed brick walls and hardwood floors. "How did you discover this place?"

Tendo dabbed the side of his mouth with a linen napkin. "I know Canary Wharf well. I grew up not too far from here, in Tower Hamlets."

"I'm actually not all that familiar with London," Vanya said. "Besides the major tourist places, I mean."

"Where did you grow up?"

"Surrey." She looked up at him. "I actually still live with my parents."

"Hey, no judgment from me. I live with my mother right now. Or, rather, she lives with me."

Vanya tilted her head. "I guess it makes it easier for them to pick our dates for us."

He laughed. "Oh, you still remember that. Mum's pretty good about it, though. She's not pushy or nosy, just overly concerned."

"You guys are close, then?"

"Yes, we are." His eyes turned to a spot on the table, which he stared at for a moment. "I'm an only child, so that definitely made our bond stronger." He looked at her again.

"How about you? How many siblings do you have?"

"I've got two big brothers. My eldest brother is a software developer and my second brother is in pharma development."

"Nordic Wind," Tendo said.

Vanya looked at him in surprise. "You've heard of it?"

"Who hasn't? Besides, my mother is from Uganda and she was very interested in the work the company is doing there."

Vanya's jaw dropped open. "Your mother is from Uganda? I was there a couple of years ago."

It was Tendo's turn to stare. "What were you over there for?"

"The first time I went was because we needed to figure out how we could get more involved in helping people get access to the new HIV medicine we'd developed. It's an amazing country. I haven't been back since my brother's wedding."

Tendo held his hand up. "Wait. Your brother got married in Uganda?"

Vanya laughed at the surprise on his face. "Yes. You know how I said we went there to work out a medicines access plan? He ended up marrying the woman who helped broker the deal."

"That's quite a story."

"I think so, too. My eldest brother married someone from Africa as well. His first wife was from Kenya, so I guess you could say we have pretty strong African connections."

Tendo took a sip from his glass of juice. "I've actually never been to Uganda. Never even been abroad. I've talked with Mum about going there with her, but you know how it is. Between studying and work, I haven't had the time yet. But it's something I want to do within the next year. I know Mum would like to see her father. He's getting quite elderly now."

"When did your mother come to the UK?"

"Ages ago. Over thirty years. Have you ever heard of the Bush War?"

Vanya shook her head and he continued. "It was the war which brought the current Ugandan president to power. Messy and ugly and plenty of atrocities. To be honest, I don't know all the details and haven't really wanted to look them up. Mum isn't keen to talk about it. Her family was mixed up in one of the political factions and they were targets, so they scraped together their savings and managed to come here. When the war ended, they decided to go back, but by then my mother was pregnant with me and didn't want to leave. So they went back and she stayed here to make a go of things with my father."

"Is your dad British?"

Tendo's face twisted. "Yes, he is British, but I don't have any contact with him. He took off to Australia when I was two years old. My stepfather raised me."

Vanya caught a tone in his voice that she couldn't quite place. She said, "Sometimes it's the people we choose to let into our lives who make all the difference. Not necessarily the ones we're related to by blood."

He looked sharply at her, then a smile spread over his face. "That's for sure. And that's why I use my stepfather's surname and confuse everyone who tries to speculate about where I'm from."

Vanya laughed. "I get that. I'm told my brothers and I have unusual names as well. My great- grandfather came over here from Norway and it's been a family tradition to give all the children Scandinavian names."

"Vanya's a very pretty name," he said.

Her face grew warm and a smile spread over her face. "Thank you."

Tendo turned his wrist over and checked his watch. "I'd better get back to my desk in case Eden sends anything through."

Vanya glanced at her own watch and was amazed at how much time had passed. "Oh, right. I'll just get the bill." She raised her hand to signal the waiter, then caught the look on Tendo's face and spoke before he could. "It's a company expense, so I'll use the company card."

He closed his mouth and nodded. "Thank you."

When she'd settled the bill and folded the receipt into her purse, they started on the short walk back to the office. Tendo fell into step beside her.

"It's been a crazy few weeks," she said. "It'll be good to ease up just a tiny bit after tonight."

"Absolutely." He frowned. "I wanted to take a couple of days off to help my mother sort out some stuff, actually, but I forgot to put in the leave application."

"That shouldn't be a problem. Update the calendar and I'll approve it. I think we could all do with a break. There's a video game I've been planning on getting for ages, but I'd put it off because we've been so busy."

He glanced at her. "Which video game?"

"Pokémon Sword."

He shook his head vigorously. "No. Absolutely not. Do not get Pokémon Sword."

She stared at him, surprised at the vehemence in his voice. "Why not? Everyone says it's a good game."

"Because I've got Pokémon Sword. You need to get Pokémon Shield so you can trade with me and I can complete my Pokedex."

He grinned as she burst into laughter. She would never have imagined that Tendo would be into video games. She said, "Since you make such a strong case, I'll get Shield instead."

"You'll love it. It's amazing. And I'm serious: you need to buy Shield and let me know so I can get hold of a Galarian Ponyta or Rapidash from you. They don't exist in Sword."

She chuckled. "Okay, okay, I will. I don't often meet a Pokémon fan."

"I'm hard core. Ever since Generation II."

"Oh yeah?" she taunted. "I go back to Generation I, Red and Blue."

"No way!" His eyes lit up as he looked at her. "Who was your Gen I starter?"

"Charmander, of course."

His eyebrows flew up. "Ooh. You like a challenge, then?"

She smiled. "Yes, I'm a woman who likes a challenge."

They continued chatting until they got up to their office floor and stood for a moment outside his office door. He rested one hand against the door frame. "Thanks for dinner. I'll just, um... sign off on the videos as they come through."

"Sure. And fill out that application for time off whenever you like. We'll all need to catch our breath a bit before we start a new twelve-week sprint."

"See you later." He went into his office and she went back to her own desk, a warm glow bathing her on the inside. It had been an amazing day. Her new department was a huge success.

As she remembered the launch, though, a shadow formed on the edges of her thoughts. The reason her team was doing so well was because of Tendo and his ideas. Her decision to back Derek's vision had been disastrous, and the only reason they'd been able to recover was because Tendo had known someone who could take over the videography.

It was wonderful to enjoy this success, but she wanted to be sure that, next time, she had more to do with it. But at least she'd insisted on bringing Pamela on board when Tendo had been set on hiring that other guy. That proved that she could do something right.

She held onto that thought and smiled as she logged onto the online gaming shop to order Pokémon Shield.

Chapter Seventeen

A FEW DAYS later, Tendo was once more in a car with Vanya. They were on their way to pay a visit to Julia Rae, the YouTube mommy vlogger who was going to be a Tymbrian Homes brand ambassador and document her journey as she moved into her new property.

The negotiations had gone smoothly and everything was agreed upon in principle. Julia had already looked over the agreement with her advisers, and Vanya and Tendo were making the trip to deliver the contract in person.

The long drive to Kent had gone by in a flash, and he was once again amazed at how much he'd enjoyed Vanya's company. They'd built on the rapport he'd felt the day they'd shared a meal at the Italian restaurant, and they had a lot more in common than he would have thought possible.

They'd been geeking out on video game talk and he'd gotten to hear more about her stays in Uganda and about how she was planning another trip to Africa. She'd be going with her brother Ragnar, who was taking his daughter to visit her grandparents in Kenya.

Vanya pulled into the driveway of a large townhouse as the GPS announced that they had reached their destination. Tendo was sorry to cut their conversation short, but he smiled as he remembered he still had the drive back to look forward to.

Vanya slid her pink moccasins off and put on a pair of knee-high boots that looked expensive and painful to wear. She straightened up and smoothed her skirt. He had no idea how she managed to walk in those high-heeled boots without breaking an ankle, but she made it look easy as she glided up the path toward the front door.

Vanya had barely finished knocking when the door swung open and a small Asian woman squealed and pulled her into a hug. Tendo recognized Julia Rae from her YouTube channel.

"Hi, Vanya! It's so good to meet you." Julia squeezed Vanya, then turned her attention to Tendo. "And you must be Tendo. Come in. It's freezing out there."

They went into the house which was clearly in the upheaval of a major move. Cardboard boxes were stacked everywhere and Tendo and

Vanya had to weave their way through the packing material to avoid stepping on several pets that dodged around. Tendo first thought there were about ten animals, but he soon realized there were two chihuahuas and two long-haired cats of a breed he couldn't place.

Two small children, clearly twins judging from their equal sizes and identical clothes, sat in the living room, popping handfuls of bubble wrap.

"Welcome to our controlled chaos," Julia said. "Well, it's chaos, but the control is debatable. Sorry about the state of things, but we're moving this weekend."

Vanya smiled. "I can't imagine how busy you must be doing all this with children and pets. Our legal team wanted in-person signatures, though, so we're grateful you let us come."

"Not a problem at all. I am super excited to be doing this!" Julia gushed. "I was telling your colleague Pamela how much we're in love with our new place. It's going to be so much fun to do this collaboration with you guys. Please sit down."

Vanya sat on a light gray Chesterfield sofa and pulled a large envelope out of her bag. She extracted the contracts and handed them over to Julia. "Here you go."

Julia took them, settled into an armchair, and began to turn the documents over. Bubbly and excitable as she was, she took a good look at every page. This was no airhead, but a smart businesswoman.

While Julia looked at the papers, Tendo watched Vanya playing peek-aboo with one of the twin toddlers. The child giggled as Vanya hid her face and peeked through her fingers.

Julia smiled at Vanya. "Kelsey loves playing peekaboo, don't you, honey?"

The other twin soon joined in the fun, and Tendo found himself smiling as well. He didn't hang out with children often, but Vanya seemed to be a natural.

One child eventually inched up to Vanya, climbed into her lap, and began examining the pendant at the end of her necklace. Julia was still absorbed in the contract, so Tendo tried to play the peekaboo game with the second twin. She stared at him with unblinking round eyes. Tendo was about to give up when the little girl suddenly broke into a grin.

The child on Vanya's lap sneezed, her head falling forward. When the little girl sat back, her face was streaked with mucus, but the greater part of it remained in a huge yellowish blob on the lapel of Vanya's designer jacket. Tendo made a face.

"Aw, sweetheart, have you got a sniffly nose?" Vanya reached into her purse for a pack of tissues and wiped the child's face. When she'd gotten the gunk off the child, she dabbed at her jacket, showing no sign of revulsion.

Words his mother had often said, but which he'd dismissed equally often, came to Tendo's mind. "Always watch how a girl behaves with children, especially if they're not hers. It will give you a real window into her heart." If Vanya Klassen could cheerfully wipe off a snotty child who left globs of mucus on her Gucci jacket, that said something very extraordinary about her heart.

Julia looked up. "This all looks great. I'm ready to sign."

She patted her pockets and Tendo handed her a pen. As she scribbled her signature on the pages, Julia said, "Can I offer you anything to drink? A cup of tea? Something else? I've only got instant coffee and basic builder's tea because, well, moving."

"Are you sure it wouldn't be too much trouble?" Vanya asked.

"No, no trouble at all. What will you have?"

"A black coffee would be great, thanks," Vanya said.

Tendo said, "Tea with milk no sugar, please."

Julia finished with the last page and handed the documents to Tendo, since Vanya's hands were full with little Kelsey. Tendo put the papers back into the envelope and slid them into Vanya's attaché case.

Vanya smiled at Julia. "You have adorable children."

Julia beamed. "Thank you so much! They normally don't like strangers, especially Kelsey, but you seem to have made a friend there.

You've really got a way with children. Do you have any yourself?"

Vanya smiled. "No, none of my own. But I babysit my nephew and nieces whenever their parents will let me."

Julia disappeared into the kitchen. The other twin followed her, while Kelsey stayed put on Vanya's lap, thumb in mouth, leaning against her chest. Seeing Vanya cradling the child stirred an ache inside Tendo that he didn't want to examine too closely.

Julia came back with the coffee and tea and they talked for a while. Julia was as charming and funny in person as she was on her YouTube channel. This brand ambassador thing was going to be great, Tendo thought.

Vanya glanced at the child in her lap. "I think she's asleep."

Julia put her mug down and stood up. "Oh, you're right. It's coming up to their naptime."

"We won't take up any more of your time," Vanya said as Julia picked Kelsey up. "Thank you so much for having us, and all the best with your move."

"Thank you, dear. It was lovely of you to come all this way. Hope you have a good drive back."

They all stood up and Vanya and Tendo went to the door. A two-hour trip out here, and the meeting was over in half an hour. But that's what networking was about. That in-person contact could go much further than dozens of emails.

They went back to the car and Tendo settled into the passenger seat while Vanya did her shoe swap. "That was short and sweet," he said.

"Yes, she seems really nice." She stuck the car key into the ignition. "I hadn't realized how close we were to Ramsgate. My grandmother had a house on the seafront. I spent some really happy summers there."

"I've never been to the seaside."

Vanya stared at him open mouthed. "Seriously?"

"Seriously. And, yes, I know the statistics and that in Britain you're never more than seventy-five miles away from the sea. But somehow we never made it there."

With the grinding hand-to-mouth lifestyle he and his mother had lived in Tower Hamlets, traveling any-where had been a distant dream. Things improved when his mother married his stepfather.

But although they were no longer destitute, there hadn't been much left over for luxuries like vacations. Once or twice Patrick had men-tioned taking a day trip out to Southend-On-Sea, but it was one of the many things he'd not managed to do before the cancer took him.

And later on when he started at the university, Tendo had been so focused on getting top grades and climbing the career ladder that the thought of going on vacation had fallen far down his priority list.

Vanya was still staring at him, her blue eyes wide. She turned away and started the car. "We're going to do something about that right now."

"What do you mean?"

"I mean we're going to the seaside. I know it's out of season and absolutely freezing and I can't promise a Punch and Judy show or a donkey ride, but you've got to see the sea."

He chuckled as he realized she was serious. She drove onto the main road and took a left turn at a roundabout.

Her eyes still on the road, she said, "There's a lovely little beach not far from here. We used to go there sometimes when we wanted to enjoy the beach without all the noise and crowds at the Ramsgate sea-front."

Tendo didn't have a desperate desire to go to the beach, especially on a cold gray day, but Vanya's keenness was charming and starting to rub off on him. He smiled. "I guess I can cross one item off my bucket list."

In a short while, they were in Broadstairs and Vanya pulled into a parking lot next to a restaurant. She said, "This is the closest place we can park, if I remember correctly. We'll have to walk from here, but it's not far." She turned her eyes to his face. "Ready?"

"I'm ready," he said.

She got out of the car and pulled her wool coat tighter against the cold wind. He followed her as she walked a short distance along the road, then turned left on a narrow path. There was a long flight of stairs between two rock faces. When they got to the bottom, Tendo gasped. They were in a secluded cove surrounded by high chalk cliffs. The gray expanse of sea stretched in front of them, impossibly wide, the white-topped waves churning like a gigantic cauldron. He took a few steps forward and turned to look at Vanya. "This is amazing!"

The wind whipped his words away and she leaned forward, strands of blond hair swirling around her face. "What?"

"I said this is amazing!"

She grinned at him and had to shout above the wind. "I know! Pity about the weather!"

He turned back to stare at the sea, his heart thrilling at the majestic power of it. It dwarfed him completely. He was a tiny, weak, insignificant ant in the face of such raw power. But the hands which had made it were even mightier. It might have been the worst possible day to go to the seaside, but to him, this was perfect.

He turned to his left. Vanya stood close by, shivering, shoulders hunched and hands deep inside her coat pockets.

He touched her arm. "Let's go back."

She looked back at him and moved a strand of hair from her eyes. It was a useless gesture because the wind blew several more back in its place. "You sure?"

"Yes, let's go before we freeze to death."

They turned back toward the stairs and he followed her, taking one last look over his shoulder before going up.

She pointed at the restaurant where she'd parked the car. "Do you mind if we get a hot drink?"

"Great idea. My treat, though."

He held the door open for her and they walked into the restaurant a moment later. A wave of warm air hit them as they stepped inside. A hostess in a white blouse and black skirt smiled at them from behind her dark wood-paneled desk. "Welcome to Captain Digby's. Table for two?"

Tendo glanced at Vanya, then back at the hostess. "Yes, please."

The hostess pulled two menus from under the counter. "This way, please." She led them to a booth in the corner. "It's not quite time for our dinner service, but we could still take your order if you would like to have a meal."

Vanya settled into her seat. "How long until dinner?"

The hostess glanced at her watch. "The kitchen opens in about twenty minutes."

Vanya turned to Tendo. "Do you want to have a meal before we head back?"

The drive to London would take at least two hours even without traffic. Tendo nodded. "Not a bad idea."

Vanya spoke to the hostess. "Okay, we'll stay for dinner. For now, could I have some peppermint tea, please?"

"I'll have some tea as well, please," Tendo said.

The waitress smiled at them. "Coming right up." She headed back toward the kitchen.

Tendo rubbed his hands together. "Thank you."

"What for?"

"For showing me the sea. I've never seen anything so incredible in my life."

Vanya grinned. "You're welcome. Not exactly beach front holiday weather, but it's always amazing."

"And to think it's only taken me thirty years to get around to seeing it."

Vanya was still smiling, but her eyes softened. "I'm glad I could see you seeing that.

Tendo's throat tightened and he picked up his menu to have an excuse to turn his gaze away. Looking into those blue eyes was churning up emotions deep inside of him just like the wind had whipped up the sea. And he didn't know how treacherous those depths could be.

Chapter Eighteen

AS VANYA watched Tendo's face while he gazed at the sea, something shifted inside her. Tendo Halloran, the ambitious content marketing genius, had been transformed into a child. She'd felt a deep gratitude as she saw the pure awe and wonder that played across his face. What a privilege to see him experience something awesome for the first time.

There were so many layers to him, and she wanted to peel them away and discover as much as he was willing to let her see. She was glad they still had this small bubble away from the world before they had to go back to London and their jobs.

They both decided on salmon with new potatoes, and the food arrived quickly.

Tendo smoothed his napkin over his lap and closed his eyes briefly before he picked up his cutlery.

Vanya had seen him do that the last time they'd shared a meal. She tilted her head as a thought occurred to her. "Were you just saying grace?"

He looked up at her. "Yes."

"You're a Christian?"

"Yes again."

She smiled. "Me too!"

His brown eyes widened and a smile spread across his face. "That explains a lot."

What did he mean by that?

As though reading her mind, he said, "You're just very different than what I would have expected, and knowing that you're a Christian makes sense of a lot of things."

"Like what?" She kept her tone light, but she was keen to know what he thought of her.

He took a sip of water and shrugged. "Given your background, I thought you'd be more... elitist and not so down to earth." He smiled. "Pamela told me how you're using binder clips to replace the broken feet on your keyboard."

Vanya laughed and her cheeks warmed up. "She told you that? It's a useful trick."

"I'd have expected you to requisition a new keyboard instead of making do like that. And some of the things you were telling me about your visits to Uganda showed me you're not as out of touch as I'd imagined. I mean, of course, it's not just Christians who want to help disadvantaged people, but it makes sense.

And you give off this wholesome vibe."

Vanya laughed out loud again. "What, like Betty Crocker? I couldn't cook to save my life."

He chuckled. "I mean you don't come across as the party girl type."

She processed his words for a moment. He'd clearly spent some time thinking about her, analyzing her personality. She liked that thought.

"So, how did you become a Christian?" she asked.

He ate a mouthful of food. "My mother is born again, and she was praying for me for years, but I didn't pay attention to anything she said. I'd seen way too much ugliness in the world to want to believe in any kind of God, let alone one who was supposedly loving and yet let all those things happen.

"Then she met my stepdad. He was this big tough Irishman who'd done time in jail for assault. That was all behind him by the time they met. While he was in prison, the chaplain preached to him and he turned his life around. So, when he talked to me, I'd listen. He was this big tough guy who'd had all of life's hard knocks, but he said God had helped him through."

He looked at Vanya. "I thought God was only for weak people who needed a crutch to lean on. My dad helped me see that God is there for me as well. As tough and as strong as I thought I was—and I was nothing compared to my dad—I still needed God in my life."

"Sounds like an amazing man."

Tendo looked down for a moment, then back up at Vanya. "He was. He went to be with the Lord when I was eighteen, soon after I got my acceptance letter to the university. It was thanks to his influence that I'm doing what I'm doing now and I'm not just another statistic, given my background."

Before she knew what she was doing, Vanya reached out and curled her fingers around Tendo's hand. The shock in his face mirrored her own, but he didn't take his hand away. Instead, he squeezed her hand and warmth spread inside her like smooth honey.

Dear Lord, I'm falling for this guy! She withdrew her hand and turned her eyes down to her plate, hoping that her face wasn't as red as it felt.

After an awkward silence, Tendo spoke. "What about you? How did you become a Christian?"

"It was my brother Ragnar and his first wife who started taking me to church. She's passed away now, but I spent a lot of time with them the year before I went to the university. Hanging out with them was nicer than being at home where my mother was on my case about... stuff."

It still hurt Vanya to think about that summer. Jessica had always nagged her about losing weight, but it had been particularly bad that year. Visiting Ragnar's home had been a welcome escape, and while she was there, she went to church with him and his wife. Hearing about a God who loved her unconditionally had fallen like rain on parched earth, and Vanya had clung to the Gospel as soon as she understood what it meant.

She poked at a piece of fish on her plate. "It's not a spectacular conversion story like yours. There wasn't much change in my day-to-day life, but I definitely wouldn't be where I am today either if I hadn't become a Christian back then."

She looked up to find Tendo's eyes on her. He smiled. "It's a beautiful story. We all need Jesus, whether you're a fatherless urchin on a sink estate in Tower Hamlets—"

"Or a billionaire's daughter in Virginia Water," she finished. "There's still a gap that nothing and nobody else can fill."

They carried on with their meal, lingering long after the waiter had taken their empty plates away, until Vanya sighed, thinking of the many miles still ahead of them. "We'd better get going. We've got a while yet to drive, but I think we may have escaped the rush hour traffic."

They stepped outside. The wind had died down and a pale moon shone in the dark sky.

Tendo looked across the parking lot and turned back to Vanya. "Do you mind if I take a moment to look at the sea again?"

"No, go ahead. Do you want to go back down to the beach? The stairs are probably hard to see now and I wouldn't want to risk it, but there's a lookout point behind the restaurant."

"The lookout point sounds good."

"This way." She walked ahead of him on a path that went behind the restaurant and past the terraced eating area popular with guests during the summer. A few yards on, they came to a paved area at the edge of the cliff, with a metal railing guarding the steep drop-off. Vanya moved next to a coin-operated telescope that looked out across the bay. The moonlight gave the waves an unearthly silvery glow.

Tendo stepped beside her, leaning his elbows on the railing. She was aware of his presence even without looking, like an invisible magnetic pull. He stared out at the water for a long time. She stayed silent as well, not wanting to interrupt whatever impulse had drawn him back here.

Suddenly, she whirled to look at him. He was humming. Then he started to sing, the melodic and rich tones of his voice filling the air. Her skin tingled with goosebumps she knew had nothing to do with the cold winter air. "O Lord my God, when I in awesome wonder consider all the work thy hands hath made. I see the stars, I hear the rolling thunder, thy power throughout the universe displayed."

He turned to face her and gestured with his hand. He wanted her to join in. She could barely hold a tune in a bucket, but she sang with him, and her unsteady warbling didn't matter. His magnificent voice held hers up as the hymn rang out. "Then sings my soul, my Savior God to thee, how great thou art, how great thou art."

The song ended. She stared at him, breathless and exhilarated, her heart pounding.

Tendo smiled at her. "I needed to do that. I'm ready to go if you are."

With the strains of his song still echoing in her heart, she nodded and they walked back toward the parking lot.

Chapter Nineteen

VANYA SAT back in her chair and listened as her team riffed off each other, tossing ideas back and forth for the next twelve-week sprint of their content marketing plan. It was astonishing how well the group had gelled together.

Traffic to the Tymbrian Homes website and social media was at an all-time high, and the sales department was hiring new staff members to deal with the upswing in new leads. Vanya no longer needed to chase down people from the other departments to do interviews and provide material for her team to use.

She broke in after Pamela had finished speaking. "All right, so we will go ahead and commission drone footage of the country clubs and golf courses. I'm not sure whether we can do the same thing for the residential properties, though, because people may not like the idea of their homes and neighborhoods being filmed and published online. We'll need to follow that up with our legal and customer relations teams."

Tendo raised his hand. "I'll do that."

She smiled at him. "Cool. And we can also green light the customer testimonials. Pamela, could you organize a call-out to our mailing list and arrange to follow up with phone calls next week? Melissa, you'll need to help with that."

Tendo looked at Vanya. "Shall Eden do the videography?"

"I wanted to have a word with you about that in just a minute." She turned to the rest of the team. "Thanks everyone. We're done here for now."

Vanya shut the door after they left. She turned around to face Tendo. "I haven't heard anything from Derek, and I'm going to terminate his contract. But first I'd like your input on the content he's already made. It doesn't fit in with our current strategy but maybe we could repurpose it and use it for something else. I was thinking we'll pay him for services already rendered and ask Eden whether she's able to continue working for us."

Tendo rubbed his chin. "We've got several months of work for Eden if she's free to take it."

Vanya nodded. "She can get started with filming the country clubs, and as soon as we've got clearance and permissions for the video testimonials and drones taking aerial footage of the homes, she can tackle that as well."

"Shall I tell Eden to be on standby for a bunch of commissions coming her way?"

Vanya gestured with a mock salute. "Make it so, Number One."

He grinned at what had become their inside joke ever since they'd discovered they were both fans of Star Trek: The Next Generation.

He stood up to leave. Vanya's heart thudded. She hadn't only asked him here to talk confidentially about Derek. There was something else she wanted to ask, but her mouth had gone dry. As his hand reached out for the doorknob, she finally conquered her hesitation. "Tendo?"

He turned to look at her and she cleared her throat. "I, um... I bought Pokémon Shield and it's a great game. I was wondering if you're still interested in doing a trade or maybe playing in versus mode?"

Relief washed over her body as he grinned. "Awesome! Yeah, I'd love to."

"Maybe we could meet up one evening or, um, just online if you'd rather do it that way."

He nodded, still smiling. "I'm totally up for that. Actually, I'm not doing anything tomorrow. Or maybe that's too soon?"

"No, tomorrow's fine," Vanya said quickly. It would be perfect, and she could avoid another one of her mother's parties.

"Where shall we meet?" he asked.

"My mother's having guests over, so my place is out."

"We could meet at my place. Shall we say one o'clock? I'll organize lunch and you can just bring your console and prepare to get toasted."

"Oh, I'm not sure about that," she said with a smile. "You might just have to eat humble pie for your tea."

He laughed and walked out of the room.

Vanya went back to her desk and spent the next five minutes failing to read her emails as she sat with a large smile on her face.

Chapter Twenty

As SOON as he left Vanya's office and his pulse settled back to normal, doubts began to assail Tendo. He kept his face neutral while he stared at his computer screen and tried to look busy.

He should have turned her down and made some excuse to avoid meeting her. And yet he was greedy for more time with her, to hear her laugh, to get closer to her and see more of the funny, sweet and quirky woman under the cool, professional facade.

Had he just made a huge mistake? He could pretend that all tomorrow meant to him was two friends hanging out together, being geeks over a computer game. But that was a lie.

Vanya wasn't just a friend. She was his boss. Worse than that, his CEO was her father. And he was spending every day fighting a losing battle against his growing attraction to her. It was hard enough hiding it at work, where their colleagues provided a buffer. If they were alone together away from the office, how would he keep himself from saying or doing something that would make her lose respect for him or hate him?

Lord, what should I do? he prayed silently.

His single-minded focus up until now had been to build his career. He never wanted himself or his mother to live through the poverty they had experienced while he was growing up. He had intentionally avoided romantic entanglements so he could pour all his energy into becoming financially secure. If you don't dabble by the poolside, you can't fall in the water, was his reasoning. He'd kept himself so busy at work that he hadn't spent enough time with anyone to get beyond a surface-level attraction.

Until Vanya.

Could there be a reason why she was in his life right now? Once again, he asked God the question that had been hanging in his mind for weeks. *Lord, is this your doing, or something I need to resist?* There was no immediate answer.

With an effort, he forced his mind to focus on the emails he needed to write.

Tendo knew he was in danger the moment he opened his apartment door to Vanya the next day. He'd only ever seen her looking professional in her tailored business outfits. But now, in dark jeans and a pale blue sweater with her long blond hair hanging loose, she looked softer and more feminine. It would be all too easy to forget that she was his boss.

He smiled and stepped aside from the doorway. "Come in. You're just in time for lunch. I've got soup and sandwiches, so we shall eat like kings."

"Thanks," she said, walking past him. She pulled a backpack off her shoulder. "I've got my console in here."

"Great. We'll set it up after we've eaten." He followed her as she stepped into his living room and wondered what she thought of his apartment.

When he'd told his mother he had a female guest coming to visit, she'd grinned at him and said, "What did I tell you? You need your space." Enid had blitzed the apartment until it was spotless, then gone to spend the day with one of her friends. She had wanted to make lunch as well, but Tendo had insisted on doing that himself.

He served up two bowls of butternut squash soup and ham hock sandwiches. Vanya's eyes widened as she tasted a spoonful. "This is delicious! Did you cook this?"

He smiled. "Thank you. Yes, I did."

She ate another spoonful. "I'm impressed. I can barely boil water in a kettle. You actually made this with ingredients? I mean, it's not from a carton?"

Tendo laughed. "Yes, I used ingredients. It's pretty easy to do. Just put them together, boil it up and stick it in the blender."

"Where did you learn to do that?"

"Jamie Oliver. Yes, really. Don't judge me, but when I first watched one of his shows, it showed me that a regular bloke could cook. I find it relaxing."

She emptied her bowl and eagerly accepted a refill.

"Dessert?" he asked, when they'd both finished eating.

"Maybe later, thanks. I'm stuffed and I want to see your gaming setup now."

"I'll put these in the kitchen and then get your console hooked up." He got to his feet and picked up their empty bowls.

She stood up as well. "Why don't I clear up while you do all the techie things? Just go ahead and grab my Switch."

"Okay, sure." He watched her gather the crockery and head into the kitchen before he remembered he was supposed to be setting up a gaming session. He found her Nintendo Switch in her backpack and began to hook up all the cables.

A few minutes later she came back into the living room. He looked up at her. "Almost done here. I've brought out my computer monitor and connected your Switch to that. Mine's hooked up to the TV, unless you want to swap. I've got an extra controller if you need one. Bear with me a minute while I get you connected to the WiFi."

She sat down next to him on the sofa. "What shall we do first? Trade or a versus battle?"

He looked at her and grinned. "Let's battle each other. I'd like to see what you're made of."

She smiled back. "It's on."

They started the game, and Tendo sent out a Pikachu as his first combat fighter. He raised his eyebrows, taken aback at the opponent Vanya chose to use against him. A stab of disappointment hit him. He'd expected her to make a smarter choice. She should have known better if she'd been into Pokémon as long as she claimed.

He hesitated before speaking. "Are you sure you want to fight my Pikachu with your Seaking? Pikachu's an electric type—oh." He stopped short at the text that flashed on the screen, then turned to look at Vanya. She had a wide grin on her face. "Your Seaking has lightning rod."

"Yup," she said. "So your electric type moves will have no effect."

"Oh, sneaky," Tendo said. His disappointment disappeared as he realized how clever her choice actually was. They began the battle and he grimaced as she took out his Pikachu with two moves.

"Fine. Let's see how you'll do against this." He sent out a powerful grass-type Pokémon that he knew would give him the advantage over Vanya's water-type Seaking. Once again, he was surprised when she chose not to switch out her fighter.

He quickly understood why when she defeated his Venusaur with her first strike. He pointed at the screen. "What? Your Seaking knows a bug-type move? That's insane!"

Vanya threw her head back and laughed. "Gotcha!"

"That's completely ridiculous. What am I supposed to do if I can't use electric or grass types against it?"

She shrugged and tilted her head. "Oh, I don't know. Maybe lose?"

Tendo laughed. "No way. I'm not going down that easily. Come on." They went on with the battle, but she easily overhauled the rest of his team.

He slapped his pillow. "I demand a rematch. But this time that over-powered Seaking of yours is banned."

Vanya laughed. "No way! It's my secret weapon. Maybe not so secret anymore."

"Fine. If I can't beat you I'll join you. Max raid battle?"

She saluted him with her controller. "Let's do it."

They teamed up and played together, then traded some of their Pokémon. Finally, Tendo sat back. "I'm convinced. You're a Pokémon master. Would you like to play something else?"

"What other games have you got?"

He pointed at a tall narrow shelf next to the TV. "Everything I've got is over there."

She stood up and walked over to the shelf and browsed through the boxes. He took full advantage of the opportunity to look at her while her back was turned. He'd been worried about being in danger of falling for her. But now he was way past the warning signs and deep in peril.

He'd let himself see yet another side of her and it drew him to her even more.

He blew out a slow breath as he faced the truth. Vanya was unlike anyone he had ever met. Just being friends with her wouldn't be enough. He wanted her heart, because she had his. But it was impossible.

She turned around, her finger on one of the plastic boxes. "You've got Super Smash Brothers Ultimate?"

"Want to play that?"

"Yes. I haven't tried it before."

She handed the box to him and he slotted the cartridge into his Switch. She settled herself cross-legged onto the sofa. He turned toward her as he started the game. "Have you played anything from the franchise before? The gameplay is pretty straightforward if you have."

He talked her through the basic setup and she got the hang of the controls within a few minutes. They played together against computer opponents, but they lost because he was looking at her face instead of concentrating on the game.

The next matchup went a lot better and they lost only narrowly as he managed to keep his focus on the screen. In their third game, Vanya struck the winning blow. She punched the air, then yelled in delight and threw her arms around him.

At her touch, a jolt of electricity flashed through Tendo. Heart thumping, he pushed her away on instinct. He jumped up and took a few steps across the room, then turned around. She sat rooted to the spot, her eyes fixed on him, her face pale.

He raked his hand through his hair and drew in a shaky breath. Color flooded back to her cheeks. She turned away from him and stood, her movements jerky. "I... I'd better go."

"Vanya, no." He was across the room again, standing in front of her.

She turned away from him and crouched down. With trembling hands, she pulled the cables out of her console and detached the controller.

He knelt next to her. "I'm sorry. You didn't do anything wrong, it's just me. I..." His words dried up as she continued disconnecting her Switch. She grabbed her bag and slid the console inside it, her face still averted, her long hair falling forward and keeping her features hidden.

He touched her shoulder, and she froze. "Vanya, please look at me." Slowly, she turned and looked into his face, her cheeks still flaming red, a sheen of moisture in her eyes. She clutched her backpack against her chest. He could tell she was hurt, and the thought that he had caused her pain made him forget his fear of what telling her the truth would mean.

His words poured out. "I'm sorry. I didn't mean to hurt you or embarrass you. It's just that when you hugged me, I knew that if I didn't get away, if I hugged you back, I might not stop there. We work together. You're my boss, and there's a line I'm scared to cross. It's because I've got..." He paused and drew a shaky breath. "I've got these feelings for you that I've been struggling to keep a lid on. I understand if you still want to leave. We can forget that it ever happened."

Her eyes widened as he spoke. She looked up at him for an eternity, then spoke so softly he barely heard her words. "What if I want to cross that line?"

His heart thumped crazily. Did she mean it? Did she feel the same irresistible pull of attraction he did?

His hand moved up to her face. She bit her bottom lip as his fingers made contact with her skin. She dropped her backpack onto the floor and laid a hand hesitantly on his chest. All the reasons why it was a bad idea to get mixed up with her faded far into the background, lost and forgotten, as he lowered his head and touched her lips with his.

She responded to him, kissing him back, her body leaning into his as he lost himself in the sweetness of being close to her.

When they drew apart, he scanned her face, half afraid of what he would read there. Regret? Shame? Her lips curved in a smile and he kissed them again, savoring the moment. When the kiss ended, he cradled her in his arms. Tears pricked his eyes while he held her, wondering what he had just started.

Chapter Twenty-One

ANYA DIDN'T want the moment to end as she nestled in Tendo's arms, his lips touching the top of her head. Her heart thudded loudly in her ears. She didn't know where the courage had come from to speak to him like she had, but relief washed over her as well as the sheer delight of knowing that he wanted her.

She broke the embrace and leaned back on her heels, registering for the first time that she was caught up in a tangle of cables and her backpack was under her knee.

She shifted her weight and pulled her backpack free. "I'm sorry. I've made a mess."

"I'll take that sort of mess any day." He smiled down at her, but his face soon turned serious. "Can we talk about what just happened?"

A shiver of fear shot through her as he helped her to her feet and steered her back to the sofa. She sat down and looked into his face, waiting for him to speak.

He reached for her hand, threading his fingers through hers, the warmth of his touch easing the cold grip of her anxiety. "Vanya, getting involved with anyone was the last thing on my mind. It wasn't even on my radar. Then I met you. But you're my line manager and my boss's daughter."

She swallowed past the lump that had formed in her throat. What was he saying?

He squeezed her hand and looked intently into her eyes. "I don't want to waste your time, and I don't think either of us are into fooling around that leads nowhere. I respect and care about you too much for that. Do you... do you want this? Do you want to be in a relationship with me?"

A shower of fireworks exploded inside her and she wanted to jump up and dance around the room. She contained her delight into a smile and nodded. "Yes, that's what I want. I know working together might make things awkward, but we can be discreet. Nobody has to know while we figure things out."

He smiled at her as his arm circled her waist. They shared a long, lingering kiss before he let her go. He brushed a strand of hair away from her cheek. "What do you want to do now? We haven't had dessert yet."

"I don't know. I'm kind of overwhelmed. I mean I'm happy but it's...

a lot." She searched his face and prayed he'd understand. "Do you mind if we call it a day?"

"Of course not. Can I call you later?"

She smiled. "I'd like that."

Vanya drove back home in a delicious daze. Tendo liked her! This incredibly talented man, whose inner strength she admired so much, saw something worthwhile in her. He more than liked her. They were actually dating.

She didn't want to ruin the moment by thinking of the implications right now, especially since he worked for her father. That was the real challenge: what this would mean for their work. And now she was doing exactly what she hadn't wanted to do and thinking about the possible fallout of dating him.

Did Tymbrian Homes have a policy on workplace relationships? There was a couple in Sales who were married. Surely that meant it should be okay.

Vanya was navigating the roads in her neighborhood sooner than she'd have thought possible. The large circular driveway at home was full of cars, reminding her that her mother was hosting a party today. She parked her car and stepped out, planning on going straight to her little bungalow.

She was still walking on air and didn't want to descend back to earth just yet, but stay wrapped up in a cloud and the memory of Tendo's arms around her. As she crossed the driveway, the front door opened and Derek stepped out. He froze in mid-stride when he saw her and raised his hand. She waved back and continued walking, but he called out to her.

"Vanya, hang on. Have you got a moment?" He jogged toward her. Groaning inside, she stopped and pivoted to face him, hand resting on her hip. He reached her and smiled. "I thought I'd see you here earlier. How are you doing?"

"I'm okay, thanks. You?"

"Great. I owe you an apology, though, about the videos. I'll drop by your office on Monday and we can work out what the next steps are with the video series."

Vanya stared at him, her mouth hanging open. That was all he had to say after ditching her just before an already tight deadline and staying out of contact for weeks? "Derek, you left us in a really difficult position when you took off like that. We had to scramble to get our content together in time. Thankfully, we found somebody who was able to deliver what we needed."

He shuffled from foot to foot, hands in his pockets. "I said I was sorry. It was a real emergency with my grandmother, and I needed to stay longer than I'd planned. She lives in a remote village in the Alps and internet access was patchy."

Vanya held up her hand. "It's over now, Derek. Someone from my office will be in touch during the week to settle on what we owe you and close out the contract."

His brows lowered. "Close out the contract? I thought we had an agreement that I was going to deliver videography services for Tymbrian Homes."

She crossed her arms and held her ground. "Our contract ended with the batch of videos that you produced. We won't require any further services from you."

"I thought you had a long list of projects you wanted done. Are you hiring somebody else to do that?"

Vanya frowned. Why was he so desperate to do this work for her? He couldn't be short of money. Not with the trust fund he was rumored to have. That wasn't her problem, though. "Bye, Derek."

His face darkened, but cleared suddenly and he smirked. "Talk to you soon. Maybe sooner than you think." He turned on his heel and sauntered away.

Chapter Twenty-Two

VANYA STARTED Monday morning on a high. She and Tendo had texted each other throughout the weekend, and it was delicious to see him this morning, although they couldn't do more than keep things to a strictly professional basis. Vanya was settling back at her desk after the morning stand up meeting with her team when Suzy breezed in.

"Hi, Vanya. Do anything interesting this weekend?"

A blush heated up Vanya's cheeks, although she knew there was no way

Suzy could know what had happened. "I just chilled out."

Suzy stepped forward, arms crossed. "I just thought I should tell you that I came across something I think you ought to see. I don't know when this happened or how it got out there. Maybe you already know about it?"

What was she talking about? Vanya stared at Suzy, failing to connect the woman's words into anything that made sense.

Suzy said, "Here, I'll show you. Could I just borrow your computer for a minute?"

"Okay." Vanya stood up, making room for Suzy to come around her desk.

Suzy opened an internet browser and typed in the YouTube address, then entered a query in the search box. Vanya's heart lurched as her own face came on the screen. Suzy clicked on the video and the world went into slow motion as Vanya watched herself fall to pieces in front of the gala banquet from several months ago. She knew she ought to stop the video, but her hand would not move. It came to an end as she ran off the stage to loud murmuring from the audience.

Vanya's mouth was dry and she stared at the screen for several moments. Her gaze flew to Suzy. "When did you see this?"

Suzy's eyes glittered although her lips were turned down. "Someone brought it to my attention. What on earth was going on, Vanya? This doesn't seem to have been that long ago."

Vanya looked at the screen again. She didn't recognize the account name of the person who had uploaded the video. But even if she tried to contact them or get YouTube to take it down, that wouldn't make any difference. It had happened at a public gathering and there had been no filming restrictions. Anyone could have taken that footage and uploaded it.

She turned back to look at Suzy, who was watching her intently. Vanya sank into her chair. "Thanks for letting me know."

Suzy stared at her a moment longer, as though waiting for her to say something else. When Vanya remained silent, Suzy said, "Well, dear, let me know if there's anything you need me to do. Take care, hun." She flashed a smile and walked out of the office.

Vanya looked at the screen again. The video had over three million views and half a million people had "liked" it. Fifty thousand people had given it a thumbs down, so that was something, at least. She scrolled over to the comments. Looking at them was a bad idea, but they drew her like a moth to a flame. Row after row of misogynistic, expletive-ridden barbs sank into her, but she kept on reading.

She looked up with a start. Tendo stood in her doorway staring at her, his eyebrows drawn together. "What's wrong?"

She let out a laugh that sounded more like a sob and gestured at her computer screen. "Just reading comments from my fan club."

He closed the door behind him and crossed the room in two strides. He leaned forward and glanced at the screen, his face clouding over. Turning back to Vanya, he held out his hand. "Come here."

Her chair thudded against the wall as she shoved it back. She rushed around her desk and into his arms. She had thought she was going to cry, but she fought back the tears, drawing strength from him as he held her close.

After a moment he asked, "Do you want to talk about it?"

She nodded and took a deep breath, blowing it out slowly. "It's a bit of a long story. When I was eighteen, in my gap year I volunteered as an intern with an organization that helps women and children living in poverty in developing countries. I got to work alongside the organization's founder. She let me shadow her and gave me little jobs to do. She was full of encouragement, telling me that she could see a lot of potential in me and couldn't wait to see what I was going to do with my life. I thought of her as my mentor.

"Anyway, I left to start university, but we always kept in touch. I volunteered there one more summer and sent regular financial contributions. This year, my brother's company was looking for a new organization to partner with to help more people in developing countries get access to

HIV treatment. It seemed like this particular agency would be a great fit. I got in touch with my mentor and came up with a plan about how the partnership would work. We were supposed to announce our partnership at this gala dinner where my mentor was guest of honor. Just before I was due to give my speech, I overheard her talking to one of her colleagues about me. She said—"

Vanya's voice faltered. "She said I was mediocre and average, and the only reason she'd been interested in me back then was because of my family and how my connections could help build her network."

The tears Vanya thought she'd held back trickled down her face, and Tendo pulled her close again. She drew a ragged breath and struggled for control, speaking against his chest. "I had to give a speech within the next five minutes and introduce this woman to the guests. I was supposed to say how I'd worked with her for over a decade and had personal experience of how dedicated she was and how she'd been a mentor to me. And I just couldn't. I completely lost it, and now someone's gone and plastered it all over the internet."

He stroked her hair. "I'm so sorry, Vanya. I knew there had to be something behind that video, but I had no idea."

She drew back and stared at him. "What, you've seen it before?"

He nodded. "A few weeks ago."

She facepalmed. "Has everyone in this department seen it?"

He winced. "I know everyone in our team has." She made a face and he reached out and held her shoulders. "But it doesn't make any difference at all to people who know you and have worked with you. And nobody else's opinions matter. Certainly not some randoms on the internet. We've all had a bad day at the office before. We're only lucky that the press weren't there to see it."

Vanya sighed. "It's not the video that bothers me the most, although that stinks. But seeing it just reminds me of what I heard her saying. And there's a part of me that wonders whether it's not actually true."

"You know it isn't true."

Vanya turned around and walked toward the window, staring out at the glass-fronted skyscrapers and the river Thames glinting far below. She hated how needy she was sounding, as though she were fishing for reassurance. She was being pathetic and sad, trying to get her boyfriend, her deputy at work, to pat her on the head and tell her she was good at her job. She drew herself up and faced Tendo again. "Thanks. Onward and upward, right?"

He looked as though he wanted to say something, but she interrupted him. "Did you find out from the legal department what our options are about taking drone footage of the residential properties?"

Tendo stared at her for a moment, then said, "Yes. I wanted to talk to you about that."

"Okay, let's hear it." Relieved that he was going along with her bid to drop the subject of the YouTube video, she went behind her desk and sat in her chair. Tendo pulled up a chair across from her and started to talk about his exchange with the legal team and what it meant for their content ideas.

Intrusive thoughts barged into Vanya's head, fracturing her concentration. Seeing that video raised the specter of Maria's poisonous words. Did Tendo think she was mediocre at her job? What did he think about how she'd been given this position even though on paper he deserved it better? She'd sneaked a look at his resume and his LinkedIn profile. His professional background and achievements were stellar.

Her father would have known exactly how well-suited Tendo was for the job. He should be the one on this side of the desk, not her. She remembered how her father had told her to look at the proposal for the new department, a proposal Tendo had created. The only reason she was here was because her father had passed Tendo over and handed her this job on a platter. Maria Sifu was right.

Tendo finished what he was saying and waited for Vanya to respond. Her face was turned toward her planner and she had a pen in her hand, but she hadn't written any-thing down.

She finally looked up at him. "Um, okay. So…" She threw her pen down and rubbed her temples. "Sorry. Do you mind if we talk about this later?"

"Sure." Was she still upset about the video? He wanted to say some-thing else, but nothing he could think of felt right. She was his girl-friend now. He should be able to comfort her. Shouldn't that come naturally? He reached out for her hand and closed his own around it. Her fingers were cold. She looked up at him, her lips pressed together in a tight smile.

"I'll get back to work," he said. "Dinner later?"

"Yes. Thank you." She squeezed his hand and he pressed her fingers to his lips before he left the office.

Suzy was walking past as he stepped out of the doorway. She paused and looked at him with arched eyebrows. "Tendo's having a closed-door conference with the boss? I never had that privilege when I was your line manager."

She tapped a black lacquer-tipped finger on her chin. "But then again, I'm not the company owner's daughter. And, besides, climbing the ladder horizontally is a time-honored strategy. I just never thought it was your style, although I admit Vanya is cute."

She smirked, and white hot rage boiled inside him. He had no comeback for her and she turned around and strolled down the hallway.

Chapter Twenty-Three

VANYA HAD just kicked her shoes off and dropped her keys in the entryway of her home when someone knocked at her door. She glanced at her watch. It was close to eleven at night. She couldn't imagine the security guard allowing anyone else into the compound at this time, so it was probably someone from the main house.

She opened the door.

Her father stood there. "Good, you're still up. I heard your car coming in. You've been out late. Burning the midnight oil at work?"

Vanya had just had dinner with Tendo, but didn't want to mention that to her father. "Anything going on?"

"I'd like a word, if you don't mind."

Vanya let him in and followed behind as he walked into her living room and sat in an armchair. "I haven't been here in a while. Lovely painting." He motioned toward an abstract picture she'd hung on the wall.

"Thanks." Surely he hadn't come here at this time to compliment her decor?

Karl leaned forward in his chair. "I wanted to speak to you before tomorrow. I've had a long talk today with Derek Coleman-Baines. I understand there's been some friction concerning his services."

So, that's what this was about. Vanya crossed her arms. "I'm terminating his contract. He bailed out on us when we were trying to get our content ready in time for the groundbreaking ceremony. He disappeared with no explanation and no way to reach him, so we found somebody else to fill in. She did a great job, so we're planning on working with her going forward."

Karl pursed his lips. "That was a bit hasty. Have you already sent the termination notice?"

An uncomfortable twinge twisted her gut. "Hasty? What do you mean?"

"Like I said, I spoke with Derek today. They had a family emergency, a health scare, and he had to spend time with his ailing great aunt."

"I thought it was his grandmother. And don't they have phones and internet in Switzerland? The least he could have done is get in touch all the time he was away."

Karl stood up. "Derek's father is a close business associate of mine. Ending Derek's contract would put me in an awkward position, so I'd rather you didn't."

Vanya blinked rapidly and shook her head. "What? Even before he took off, the one video he delivered wasn't usable."

"I saw that video. There was nothing wrong with it. I thought it was a highly professional piece of work."

Vanya raked her hands through her hair. "It was okay as a promotional profile piece for you, but it didn't fit the brief we gave him about giving new customers information about Tymbrian Homes."

Karl walked over to the painting and leaned forward to examine it. "Then give him a better brief and monitor his team more closely to make sure they fulfill it. It sounds to me that the issues you had with him could all be resolved with better communication." He turned around to face her. "There is no need to burn bridges and upset delicately balanced business relationships just because you got your wires crossed. This isn't a suggestion, Vanya. It's a directive from your CEO and board chairman. Derek stays."

Vanya couldn't believe what Karl was saying. "But if I keep Derek on, I'll have to drop Eden. With the rates Derek charges, we don't have the budget to keep two videographers. You want me to let go of Eden, who stepped in and rescued our launch, and rehire the person who let us down in the first place?"

"I want you to give Derek the benefit of the doubt and iron out the wrinkles in your collaboration."

"The issues we had with him are a bit more than just wrinkles."

Karl walked across the room and picked up a metal ornament, examining its contours. "Were the videos Derek made technically inferior? Was their quality poor?"

"No, but they weren't what we needed and he made a huge fuss about making the changes we wanted."

Karl put the ornament down and shot her a piercing look. "A competent manager should be able to handle her contractors and make them deliver the work required. You admit Derek is capable of doing the work. You need to get better at making him give you what you need. This is a management issue, Vanya, not a staffing problem."

She flinched at his words. Now he was blaming her for Derek's failures? She didn't trust her voice to answer him back. He walked past her toward the front door, then turned and spoke over his shoulder. "Derek will stop by your office tomorrow. I expect you to make it clear to him that his contract is still running. Good night."

Vanya stared at the door for several moments after Karl left, then dropped into a chair. What had Derek said to pull this off? She remembered his smirk the last time they had spoken and how he told her he might be seeing her sooner than she expected. He had been planning to do something like this. She clenched her fists.

How could she have ever considered him attractive and even had a crush on him once? And now she was going to have to tell her team that he was back and find some way to explain the U-turn.

Her stomach tightened. What would Tendo think?

Chapter Twenty-Four

DEREK TURNED up at Vanya's office bright and early the next morning before she'd had a chance to tell her team he was back. She wished desperately that she'd sent Tendo a text at least. This is what she got for procrastinating.

Derek's button-down poplin shirt looked as though he had just grabbed it off the store rack. He smiled, displaying the dimples that had once sent Vanya and her school-mates into fits of giggles. Today, though, his self-assured good looks did nothing for her.

He eased himself into an armchair. "You're looking lovely as usual today. You were expecting me, I understand?"

She didn't return his smile. "Yes. Not this early, though."

"I thought I should display my keenness to jump into the next project." He leaned forward, the smile gone now, his gaze intense. "We began this project on the wrong foot, and I'm very eager to put things right. Can we wipe the slate clean and have a fresh start?" He held out a hand, which she refused to take.

"I don't appreciate being strong-armed into continuing with the contract. Going to my father like that was a low move, Derek."

His hand hung in the air for a few moments longer before he drew it back. "Fair enough. I'm sorry I had to do that, but your father understands a key concept. Relationships are very important in business, Vanya, and I didn't want an uncomfortable situation between my family and yours. My continuing this contract really is the best way forward. We will, of course, do our best to stick to the project brief you give us. So, what do you say? Clean slate?"

"Only if you deliver the work we want when we want it."

"Absolutely. Just tell me when we can meet up to go over the projects you have for us."

She turned to her computer and searched for the design brief Tendo and Pamela had written for Eden. Her heart weighed down in her chest like a heavy stone as she found the document and clicked on "print." She stood up to retrieve the printed pages and handed them to Derek. He took them from her, brushing his fingers against her hand.

Vanya pulled her hand away. "That outlines what we want and our deadlines. It's pretty straightforward. I'll need you to get back to me as soon as possible with a project timeline. I'll expect progress updates every Monday."

He crossed his legs and smirked. "I love the take-charge attitude. Instructions received loud and clear."

She glared at him and went back to her desk. "I've got a staff meeting now. I'll be waiting for your timeline."

He stood up. "Aye-aye, captain. I'll speak to you soon." He smiled again and walked out of the room.

Tendo came in seconds later, jerking his thumb over his shoulder. "What's he doing here?"

Vanya rubbed the back of her neck and sighed. "I should have told you yesterday, but I found out late."

He frowned. "Told me what?"

"Derek's working for us again."

Tendo blinked rapidly. He shook his head. "What?"

"My father insists we keep Derek on."

Tendo opened his mouth, then turned his face away and took a few steps toward the window. Facing Vanya, his arms crossed, he asked, "What about Eden? I sent her the project briefs yesterday for the testimonials and country club filming."

Vanya groaned. "Derek's going to be working on those." She picked up her phone. "I'll let her know."

"I can do it," Tendo said. "She's my friend and I brought her in."

She looked up at him. "I get that, but I still think it's my responsibility as team leader to give her the news."

Tendo shrugged and walked across the room. He stood facing the window, shoulders stiff. She dialed Eden's number but the call went through to voicemail. Vanya put the phone down. It wouldn't be right to inform her over the phone. "She's not picking up. I'll call her later."

Just then, Pamela, Melissa, and Omar appeared at the door for their daily stand-up meeting. Vanya walked around her desk and the group gathered in a messy circle to give her a quick update on what they were working on.

She looked around at everyone. "Hi, guys. Before we start, I need to share a bit of news with you. We're going to be working with Derek again on our video projects. So, Pamela, and Melissa, I'll copy you in on all our email communications. He'll be sending a project timeline soon telling us how he expects to carry out the work."

Pamela, Omar, and Melissa exchanged glances, but Tendo kept his eyes turned toward the floor and his arms tightly crossed.

Pamela asked, "We're not going to be working with Eden anymore?"

"Not on our current projects. Okay, I'd like to hear everyone's updates. Shall we start with you, Omar?" Vanya injected a brisk and businesslike tone in her voice. It sounded false to her own ears, but she didn't want to dwell on the Derek issue. Making it a talking point might cause an atmosphere when they were working with him. The best thing to do was present it as a done deal and get everyone to roll with the changes.

She listened as the team members spoke briefly about what they were working on that day. There was none of the banter that usually punc-tuated their meetings. When it was Tendo's turn to speak, he barely looked at her. The team members exited her office quietly when the stand-up was over.

Vanya sank into a chair and pressed her hands to her mouth, praying silently. She picked up her phone. She'd better get it over with and talk to Eden.

This time, the videographer answered at the second ring. "Hello?"

"Hi, this is Vanya from Tymbrian Homes. Do you have a moment?"

"Hi! I was just about to get in touch with Tendo. I need some more details about the drone filming project so we can apply for the right paperwork from the aviation authority. We'll have—"

"Eden, sorry to interrupt you." Vanya's heart sank to hear the enthusiasm in the other woman's voice. "There's no easy way to tell you this, but we're going to have to pull the plug on that project."

There was a sharp intake of breath and a long pause before Eden spoke. "Pull the plug? Are you withdrawing the contract?"

"Yes. I'm really sorry. It's nothing to do with the quality of work you've done. Some internal changes in our office have made it necessary for us to do this."

"Okay," Eden said. "Well, it's nice of you to tell me before I incurred even more expenses preparing for your project."

Vanya imagined she could hear an edge of sarcasm in Eden's voice that belied the polite words. "If we've left you out of pocket, of course we'll reimburse you. Please send an invoice through and we'll deal with it straight away."

"I'll do that. Goodbye, Vanya."

As Vanya ended the call, a message bubble popped up on her computer, alerting her that a new email had arrived. It was from Derek, with questions about the work assignment.

Glancing at his first two inquiries, it was clear he hadn't read the project brief in any depth. She banged her phone down and replied to Derek's email with three words: *Read the brief.* She hit "send" and buried her hands in her hair.

Chapter Twenty-Five

TENDO WAS not interested in watching the latest film adaptation of a Jane Austen novel, but Vanya was keen on it, and he was looking forward to some mindless distraction tonight after a frustrating day at work. So, he found himself standing in a large multiplex cinema holding a bag of popcorn and waiting for Vanya to finish her restroom break so they could go into the screening of *Mansfield Park*.

His patience was worn to a frazzled thread after the last few days of working with Derek Coleman-Baines. The man was a metaphorical headache and was giving Tendo a physical one that had been building up behind his eyes all day.

Derek and his team had begun filming Tymbrian Homes customers for the video testimonials, which were going to be a key part of the company's marketing materials. But after getting an email from a home-owner complaining about how Derek's team had handled her, Tendo had started insisting on being present for the filming sessions, or sending Pamela when he couldn't be there.

Babysitting Derek on top of their usual workload was taking a toll on the team, and they were now lagging behind their targets.

He glanced at his watch. Vanya had been gone for ages. Why did women take so long in the restroom, anyway? The movie was going to start soon.

"Tendo! How are you doing?"

He spun around. Nick and Miguel, who both worked in Tymbrian Homes' marketing department, were walking up to him. "Hi. What's up? What have you guys come to see?" Two thoughts flashed in his head at the same time. He'd made a blunder by choosing a theater just a few blocks from the office, and he hoped that Vanya would stay in the bathroom a while longer, until these guys were gone.

Miguel spoke around a mouthful of popcorn. "We're going to see *Sawblade IV*. Have you come to watch that, too? It's over there at Screen Four."

"No, I'm here to see Mansfield Park."

Miguel and Nick swapped glances and Nick guffawed. "Go on, man. Tell us who she is."

Heat rose up Tendo's neck. "Who who is?"

Nick leered at him. "The chick. There's no way you'd be going to see a sappy movie like that unless there's a chick involved."

Tendo shook his head and glanced behind Nick, toward the ladies' restrooms. "Can't a guy elevate his cultural horizons? Go watch your movie. I'm going to be late for mine." He turned toward the door of the screening room, praying that Vanya wouldn't show up yet. Nick and Miguel laughed again and strolled off.

Moments later, Vanya walked toward him from the ladies' room. She smiled at him and slipped her fingers into his hand. "Let's go in. I think we're just in time to catch the trailers."

He shot a quick glance over his shoulder. No sign of Nick and Miguel. His relief was shot through with guilt about not wanting to be seen with her. But after Suzy's crass comments, Tendo was hypersensitive to what people at work would say if his relationship with Vanya became public knowledge. He knew if it had been him on the outside looking in, he might have had the same suspicions as Suzy: dating the boss was a quick way up the career ladder.

Tendo blinked in the dim light of the screening room, squinting as he looked for their seats. They found their row and settled into the plush velvet chairs. Vanya interlaced her fingers with his.

He did his best to get into the movie, but the story irritated him. All he saw were entitled people running around getting into dilemmas of their own making. One of the characters reminded him of Derek, and he scowled as he thought of how he'd had to soothe the ruffled feathers of a Tymbrian Homes customer today when Derek and his crew showed up two hours late for a film-ing session. Didn't Derek realize these people were doing the com-pany a favor by agreeing to give those video testimonials? Derek be-haved as though they were extras on a movie set to act at his beck and call.

Peals of laughter burst out around the theater. Vanya giggled and turned to look at him and share the laugh. He hadn't realized something funny was happening in the movie. He pinned on a smile and turned back to the screen.

He'd avoided making any com-ments to her about Derek's performance, although each day added fresh fuel to his growing irri-tation. Derek's attitude was what grated on him the most. Tendo wouldn't have minded so much if Derek had been bad at his job yet still put in the effort to get better. But Derek acted as though he didn't care whether or not he was producing good work. Typical upper-class attitude. Every benefit of privilege and wealth had probably fallen into Derek's lap. He'd never had to hustle for anything beyond the sort of string-pulling that had landed him this contract.

And now Tendo and his team, who had nothing but their skill to recommend them and no family connections to fall back on if they failed, had to prop up this fellow who had been imposed on them. All of their jobs depended on picking up the slack that Derek left.

He glanced at Vanya. Her attention was completely on the movie. What did she think about the Derek situation? He was reluctant to complain in case it sounded as though he was criticizing her father. He didn't know whether their new relationship could take him speaking his mind about what he thought about Karl's way of doing business. He'd avoided asking her exactly how Derek had regained his contract, and she hadn't volunteered any information. As far as he knew, it had something to do with Derek's ties to one of Karl Klassen's business associates.

He shifted in his seat as a long-buried thought resurfaced. Vanya had her job because of her connection to Karl. If she had been a stranger who walked in off the street, would she be considered qualified to be heading the content marketing department of a billion-dollar property development firm? She had proven herself to be up to the task, but she was part of a system where doors were opened because of who you knew.

Could he really condemn Derek being the contracted videographer because of his links to Karl while excusing Vanya being hired? She snuggled closer and laid her head on his shoulder. His throat tightened as guilt shot through him over his disloyal thoughts.

The atmosphere around him grew heavy and he pulled at his collar.

Chapter Twenty-Six

ANYA STARED across her desk at Derek as he slouched in a chair. "This is the fifth complaint I've had about your filming crew." She stabbed a finger at her screen, where an email stood open. "This customer is withdrawing from the project. She says your team showed up late and made her do dozens of retakes."

Derek sighed. "The lateness was unfortunate, and we apologized for that. We needed to do several retakes so we could be sure we got the best possible footage."

"She also says that one of your crew shouted at her child."

"The kid was probably messing about with some of our equipment."

"But was there any reason to yell?"

Derek shrugged. Vanya glanced at Tendo, but his gaze was fixed on the notebook on his lap. She clicked on another email and turned to Derek. "This customer said your crew were trying to put words into her mouth and make her say things that weren't accurate."

Derek raised a finger. "I remember that one. We needed her to tweak just one detail so it would come across better when we edited the footage."

Vanya took a deep breath and counted to ten, exhaling slowly. "Derek, we have a serious problem. One complaint is too many. There are at least six that have come to my attention. I have to assume that for everyone who's complained, there is at least one more who's unhappy with their experience but has chosen not to express it."

"We need to produce high-quality video, so there are standards we need to keep up. The talent needs to be able to take direction from the film crew."

Vanya threw her hands up. "That's just it. These are not 'talent'. They're regular people, our customers, who are doing us a huge favor by allowing a film crew into their homes. They're giving up their time in order to give us testimonials. There's very little in it for them. We need to handle them like gold dust, not treat them as though they're hired workers."

Derek raised his eyes. "You make a very good point, actually. Working with these customers gives us major limitations, especially if people are going to act like precious snowflakes and take offense at reasonable crew directions. I've been thinking for a while that it might be a better idea to hire professional actors who can record these testimonials for us. I'm sure our turnaround time would improve a lot. We'd still use the customers' houses, if needed."

Vanya's jaw hung open while she listened to Derek. "Are you serious? Absolutely not."

His brow furrowed. "Why not?"

Vanya looked at Tendo. Was he hearing this? Tendo was watching Derek, but his expression was blank. Vanya spoke with exaggerated slowness. "Because by definition, a testimonial is coming from a real customer expressing in their own words why they're happy with the home they've bought from us. Using actors would defeat the whole purpose."

"It's standard practice to use actors. And they wouldn't be lying. They would just be delivering the words of your customers. It would still be an authentic opinion, only performed by a professional."

"No, no, no, on many levels," Vanya said. "Somebody would be sure to point out that these so-called customers are actually actors. Can you imagine how embarrassing that would be for us? Don't you remember what happened a couple of years ago when the government put out those brochures about all those people who were supposedly happy switching to the new welfare scheme? The media soon discovered they had used stock images. It's so easy for people to find this sort of stuff out."

Derek waved his hand in a dismissive gesture. "The level of scrutiny is completely different. I doubt that eagle-eyed news hounds would have the time to do reverse image searches on Tymbrian Homes' marketing materials."

"It still goes against the spirit of what a testimonial is, and it's not the way we want to operate. Even if nobody ever checks or finds out, we need to have the highest standards of integrity." Vanya looked over at Tendo as she spoke, expecting to see some backup. But he was back to studying his planner.

Derek narrowed his eyes. He was silent for a moment, then smirked. "We'll just have to run it by Karl and see what he thinks. Let him decide whether or not it's in the spirit of your advertising campaign to use professionals."

Vanya sucked in a breath. "It's not an advertising campaign. It's content marketing, and it's supposed to be authentic customer testimonials. Therefore, we get bona fide customers testifying to how happy they are to have bought a home from us. It's about building trust and using real people. We do not bring in actors to perform."

Derek leaned back in his chair, lacing his fingers behind his head. "Let's ask Karl."

Vanya's face burned. She spoke to Tendo. "What do you think?"

He shrugged. "If that's how decisions are going to be made, then let's ask Karl."

Derek grinned. "There you go. Tendo agrees. Was there anything else? I have an appointment in forty-five minutes."

Still trying to process Tendo's words, Vanya said to Derek, "No, that's all. Go ahead and leave for your appointment."

"Thank you." Derek unfolded his long frame from the armchair. "Later, then. Shall I have a word with Karl about the actor question if I run into him at the club tonight?"

"No, I'll deal with it."

"If I see him, I'll drop a word in, too. It won't hurt if he hears both sides of the argument." Derek raised his hand in a mock salute and walked out of the office.

Tendo stood up as well and headed toward the door. Vanya said, "Don't go yet. We need to talk."

Chapter Twenty-Seven

ENDO STOPPED in mid-stride and faced Vanya. Her eyebrows were drawn together, a fine crease between them.

She gestured toward the chairs where he and Derek had been sitting moments before. "What was that about?"

"What?" He knew what she was going to say and only asked as a stalling tactic. His stomach felt like lead.

"Why didn't you back me up? You've been attending some of those filming sessions and I know some of the customers have reached out to you."

"I've done what I can when I'm on site, and I've tried to make things run smoother between Derek's crew and our customers. Derek's already seen me doing that, so he's aware he needs to reel his team in."

She rested one hand on her hip. "But it would have been nice to have you speak up in here. You looked completely disengaged."

He shifted his weight from one foot to another. She was right. "Maybe I could have said more. But you explained all the customer complaints clearly and Derek didn't seem to be receptive anyway. I don't think it would have made much of a difference if I'd spoken up."

"And what about Derek's bright idea about using actors? Don't tell me you think that's a good move."

He leveled his gaze at her. "Does it matter what I think when he's going to appeal to Karl anyway?"

A flush of pink tinged her cheeks. "I expected you to give your input. That's why I asked you to attend the meeting. Whether or not it changed Derek's mind, it would have been nice to have some support."

Tendo's heart twinged. "You know you have my support."

"It didn't feel like that. What did you mean by agreeing with Derek when he said he was going to ask Karl about using actors for the testimonials?"

Tendo lowered himself into his chair again. "Like I said, there's very little point to sticking my neck out with my opinions if somebody is going to go way over my head and bring in the CEO. Derek has already made his mind up to try to get Karl's backing, so it would have been a waste of energy to try and talk him out of it."

Vanya crossed her arms. "I'm not saying I agree with Derek, but isn't that what you did?"

Tendo blinked at her. "What do you mean?"

"I mean when you took your big proposal to the board of directors about starting this department. Didn't you do that over Suzy's head?"

Heat suffused Tendo's face. "That was a completely different scenario. I didn't have any extra clout. I just wanted my proposal to get a fair hearing and not be shelved and ignored like Suzy intended."

He stood up and paced the room, trying to figure out how to collect his thoughts into words. Vanya watched him, fidgeting with a pen. Looking at her face, Tendo made up his mind. He needed to be honest with her. He crossed the room to close the office door, then went back to his seat.

"Vanya, I'm not going to lie. I'm struggling right now because there are all these hidden dynamics going on. Decisions are made in this place by mechanics I can't understand. And they are decisions that affect my ability to do my job. When I lose six hours every day because I need to make sure Derek's crew doesn't upset our customers, those are six hours I can't be doing something else."

She pushed her hands into her hair and sighed. "I know. It frustrates me as well."

"When I'm sitting at my next appraisal and I'm asked to account for how well I've reached my targets, will I be able to say I missed them because I've been spending all this extra time and energy picking up after Derek and his team?"

"I'll be doing your appraisal. I understand what you've been dealing with."

"And that's another problem." He squeezed his eyes shut and pinched the bridge of his nose. How would she take what he was going to say? "The reason you understand, the reason you see what's going on, is because we're together. We're dating, so I have your ear in a way that other people don't. And Derek has some sort of pull or hold over Karl."

A surge of emotion swept over him, thickening his voice as tears blurred his vision. "I came from nothing, Vanya. Nothing. I've fought tooth and nail and worked hard for everything I've got. That means wherever I am, I can hold my head up and be proud of what good, honest work has brought me. All this backroom wheeling and dealing goes against everything I believe in. But how can I speak up when by being close to you, I'm very much a part of it? Doesn't that make me a hypocrite?"

The color drained from her face. "What are you saying?"

He threw up his hands. "I don't know what I'm saying. But I despise this situation and the way things operate here, when Derek can freely ignore the chain of command and run straight to Karl. Derek joining our team isn't the first time Karl has imposed his choice on this department."

Vanya flinched and her hand flew to her throat. As soon as he had spoken those last words, Tendo wished he could snatch them out of the air and stuff them back inside his mouth. She stared at him, her eyes wide and unnaturally bright.

He held out his hands. "I didn't mean it to come out the way it sounded."

She shook her head slowly. When she spoke, her voice wasn't much more than a whisper. "What did you mean it to sound like?"

Tendo swallowed. He fumbled for the right words to say, knowing nothing could remove the sting of what he'd already said. "I meant that around here, Karl has the final say and all we can do is work around his decisions." Why hadn't he said that in the first place?

"Decisions like making me the manager of this department when you are better qualified for the job." Her gaze didn't drop away from his.

Tendo stayed silent. He was already deep in a hole; it was time to stop digging.

"I think you'd better get back to work." She turned her eyes back to her screen.

He stood up to leave, but hesitated. "Vanya, we can't leave things like this. I didn't express myself properly. There's a world of difference between you and Derek. You listen and you're responsive and you don't act as though you know it all. You're a great manager."

"But my father imposed me on the department when there would have been a better choice."

Tendo winced. "Please don't put words in my mouth. I didn't say that."

"But didn't you think it?" Tendo hesitated a beat too long, and Vanya's lips curved upward in a small hard smile. "Never mind, Tendo. Things are becoming very clear to me. What I don't understand is why you even want to be in a relationship with me since it goes against your principles."

"You're not being fair. I care about you and I think you're a lovely woman with a beautiful heart. My feelings for you have nothing to do with whatever else is going on in the office."

Tears welled up in her eyes. He reached out for her hand, but she pulled it away. She stared down at her lap. "I... I need space to think. Please go."

The look on her face wrenched his heart. He wanted to pull her into his arms and hold her, but he obeyed and walked out of her office without another word.

Chapter Twenty-Eight

Vanya pressed a fist to her mouth as Tendo walked away. As soon as the door closed, her body slumped forward against her desk and she didn't try to hold the tears back.

It was happening again. She had been exposed as the fraud she really was. Just like Maria Sifu, Tendo could see she didn't really deserve to be where she was. Her throat tightened as she gasped for breath.

She'd never achieved anything without getting a huge boost from her family. And this brand publishing department which was doing so well right now would never have gotten off the ground if it hadn't been for Tendo. Her department only made progress when she got out of his way and let him do what he did best.

"I despise this situation," he had said. She was a part of what he despised. He should have been the one sitting behind this desk leading this department, not her. And instead of promoting him, her father had just handed it over to her. Tendo had every right to feel cheated out of a position he deserved, one he had worked so hard for. How long would it be until his resentment spilled over to her?

But hadn't it already?

He had said that being with her, dating his line manager, made him feel like a hypocrite when he prided himself on how much he'd achieved through his own merit. There wasn't any future for them if that's how he felt. Fresh tears filled her eyes.

She remembered that afternoon in his apartment when he'd pushed her away from him. He'd said he'd done that because she was his boss and he didn't want to cross that line. Perhaps he was regretting going against his principles.

The cold hand of fear gripped her. That must be it. Everything he had said today pointed to how conflicted he still felt about being involved with her, especially since the very reason she was his boss was because she had been "imposed" on the team.

He said he cared about her, but she wanted him to respect her as well. But she couldn't expect him to respect her when every day he saw proof of how she reaped the benefits of a job she didn't deserve.

She had hoped it wouldn't matter that they worked together, that she was his boss. But it clearly did. She was in love with a man with whom she had no future. Continuing in a relationship with him was a torturous road to more heartbreak.

She drew in a shaky breath, held it for a few seconds, then breathed out slowly. After several more breaths, her tears subsided. She reached for her phone and pulled up Tendo's number.

Tendo went back to his desk, a thick fog of anguish surrounding him. He wanted desperately to go to Vanya and take back everything he had said if it would remove the pain he'd seen in her face. Why had he opened his mouth to tell her all that? Because of Derek and some worthless marketing campaign?

He sat in his chair and brought his computer screen back to life. He was supposed to be reading through some blog copy Pamela had drafted.

He opened the document and stared at the lines of text for several minutes until he realized that he'd read the same line five times, but it still made no sense to him. He minimized the window. A cup of coffee would be good, and the walk to the break room to get it would be even better.

He got to the break room to find the coffee pot empty, and went through the motions of brewing up a fresh one. As he set the water down, his phone pinged. His heart squeezed when he saw a message had come through from Vanya. He swiped across the screen, his eyes flying over the words she had written.

I think it's best that we call things off between us. I'm sorry.

She was dumping him by text? As though they were in high school? He set the phone down and gripped the counter, taking deep breaths. He fought against an urge to go to her office and demand they talk through things properly. They had known dating while working together would be a challenge. Shouldn't they try to work things out like adults? He picked up his phone and typed a reply.

Can't we talk? Let's go somewhere that's not here and try to work through things.

He hit the send button and stared at his phone, waiting for an answer to come through. It did, seconds later.

No.

He slammed his fist on the counter, making the ceramic mugs clatter. After walking up and down the room in an attempt to calm down, he typed another message.

Vanya, let's talk. It's what grownups do.

Her answer flew back a minute later.

Grownups rip off the Band-Aid. Let's be mature enough to admit it's not going to work and end it while we still have some respect for each other.

Frustration boiled up inside Tendo. How had things gone crazy so fast? It wasn't fair of her to just cut things off like that. He was about to send another message when he remembered a former colleague of his who'd been slapped with a sexual harassment complaint when his love affair with a coworker ended. Who knew what could happen if he persisted in asking Vanya to talk things through?

His stomach was in tight knots and the thought of coffee suddenly nauseated him. He turned the machine off and went back to his desk. This was exactly why he'd known he shouldn't date someone at work, and definitely not his boss.

Why hadn't he listened to the warning bells? Maybe God had been trying to get his attention to make him put on the brakes, but he'd been too caught up in his attraction to Vanya. He'd let her fill up his heart. Well, now he was going to have to pay the consequences.

An email popped up on his computer screen. He opened it and scanned the message. Another customer grumbling about Derek's crew. Tendo gritted his teeth and hit the reply button to compose yet another apologetic message.

Chapter Twenty-Nine

THE FIRST morning Vanya came to work after her break up, she had only one prayer: *God, please don't let me cry in front of Tendo.* Her throat ached as he came into her office with the rest of the team for their daily standup meeting.

Tendo appeared as keen to avoid meeting her eyes as she was to evade his, judging from how he addressed his report to every other team member but her.

Pamela was next to speak. "I just got an email from one of our video testimonial customers before I came in here. She's unhappy with how she's been handled by the filming crew, and is threatening to withdraw her consent unless she gets a written apology."

Vanya winced and sighed. As far as she knew, Derek had not carried out his intention to talk to Karl. Her father was leaving for a holiday in the Bahamas later today, and she didn't think Derek would interrupt Karl's vacation to ask him about using actors.

She had some breathing room until Karl came back, but she needed to deal with this issue before Derek trashed the company's reputation. She had to do something decisive and effective, preferably without leaning on Tendo.

"Forward the email to me, and I'll deal with it," she told Pamela.

When the meeting ended, she sent the customer a groveling email and asked her assistant to arrange for a John Lewis gift card and bouquet of flowers to follow up. The apology and gift might placate this particular customer for a while, but it was just a temporary measure. She drew a blank, though, when she racked her brain for a solution to the Derek situation.

A message popped up on her calendar app. Ringed in pink with heart emoticons, it announced what she'd rather forget: she and Tendo were supposed to have a date tonight. Why hadn't she cancelled that entry? Tears filled her eyes. He'd been planning to introduce her to his mother. She deleted the message and dabbed at her eyes with a tissue.

Every fiber of her wanted to pick up the phone and tell him she'd made a mistake and beg him to forget everything she'd said. But she couldn't do that. He had started dating her against his own principles, and that day in her office he had shown how much he was still conflicted about being with her. Even though he'd texted her about wanting to talk things through, he probably would have ended things eventually. She had only pulled the trigger first. She had to get over him.

She grabbed her phone and sent a text message to her sister-in-law Nia, asking whether Vanya could stop by tonight. Nia replied with an enthusiastic invitation, and Vanya sighed, relieved she wouldn't have to spend the evening on her own.

When five o'clock rolled around, Vanya shut down her computer and fled the office, glad to leave work problems behind her.

As soon as she got to Magnus and Nia's home, she grabbed her little nephew and immersed herself in playing with him until he was ready to go to bed. She adored everything about him: his laugh, his chubby, cuddly shape that was made for hugs, and the warm tawny skin that was a legacy of his multiracial heritage. She and Tendo could have had a baby that looked like this. Whoa, now. Where did that thought come from? She blinked away the sudden moisture in her eyes as she handed the baby to her brother.

"Come on, little guy. Time for your bath." Magnus kissed the top of his son's head and walked out of the room.

Vanya tried to avoid Nia's eyes, hoping her sister-in-law hadn't noticed her rush of emotion. But Nia wasn't that easily put off. She touched Vanya's shoulder. "Everything okay? Seems like ages since we last had a chance to talk."

Vanya was about to brush the question away, but hesitated before the words of denial came out of her mouth. She was tired of trying to hold it together all day at work, exhausted from keeping a brave and professional face and hiding the heartbreak that had made her cry herself to sleep. She shook her head. "No, I'm not okay. I split up with my boyfriend."

Nia drew a quick breath. "Boyfriend? I didn't know you were seeing anyone. I'm so sorry." She folded Vanya into a hug. "Do you want to talk about it?"

Vanya nodded and glanced at the door. "Magnus—"

"Ah, yes. I'll tell him we're having some girl time and he needs to go build a jigsaw puzzle or something." She walked out of the room.

Vanya wrapped her arms tightly around her middle. Nia was back in a moment. She sat down again in the armchair opposite Vanya. "He'll stay out of the way. What's been going on?"

Vanya sighed. "It was this guy at work. I'm his line manager. I know, I know, I was asking for trouble." She looked up at Nia. "His mother's from Uganda, by the way."

Nia's eyebrows flew up. "Really? What's his name?"

"Tendo."

"Nice solid name. What went wrong?"

Vanya shrugged. "I think I was kidding myself that it would ever work."

Nia frowned. "What makes you say that?"

Vanya fiddled with her bracelet. "We had a big fight about some guy my dad insisted we hire. He's the son of one of Dad's business associates and has been nothing but a headache. Tendo said he hates all the... he didn't actually use the word nepotism, but that's what he meant. He said he's gotten where he is through nothing but hard work and it goes against his core values to be part of a system where people get jobs and special access just because of their relationships. The way Father gave the other guy his contract and... and... the way I got my job." A tear rolled down her cheek.

Nia's mouth hung open. "He actually said that to your face?"

"Not exactly. But when I asked him if that's what he thought, he didn't deny it."

Vanya looked up at Nia. "You know the job I have? It should have been Tendo's. The department was his idea. He put together the whole concept. He's got all the qualifications and experience. But Dad passed him over and gave the job to me. It bothered me a lot at first, but then Tendo and I worked so well together, and we started dating and I thought it wouldn't be a problem. Then we had this fight, and it made me realize maybe it's a much bigger issue than I thought."

Vanya's voice shook. "The things he said reminded me so much of what I heard Maria saying. And the worst thing is, he's right. It's all true."

Nia crossed over to the sofa and sat next to Vanya. She grabbed one of Vanya's hands. "No, it's not true."

"It is. The only jobs I've ever had have been in family businesses. Tendo said he feels like a hypocrite being with me when he believes in getting ahead only through hard work and not because you happen to know the right people. So I said we'd better end our relationship. How could we ever have a future together?"

Nia squeezed her hand. "Oh, Vanya. If he really can't see past your family ties and recognize what an incredibly talented and hard-working person you are, maybe you're better off without him."

"But doesn't he have a point?"

Nia put her arm around Vanya's shoulders. "Let's talk about you first. You have a bad case of impostor syndrome."

"What?"

"Impostor syndrome. It's when you think that you don't deserve your success, or that everything you've achieved happened because of luck or good timing, and you're always afraid people are going to expose you as a fraud."

Vanya's body stiffened. She sat up and stared at Nia. "That's exactly how I feel. As though Maria and Tendo can see right through me and how I'm just a mediocre person who's been pushed into these positions because of my family connections. And it is true. You can't tell me it isn't."

"But have you done your work poorly? Have you failed to perform up to scratch at Nordic Wind or at Tymbrian Homes? Fine, maybe you did get those jobs because you're the CEO's sister or daughter or whatever. But once there, you've worked harder than anyone else and excelled at everything you've been asked to do. I've worked with you, Vanya, and I know you're anything but mediocre."

A warm glow spread through Vanya. "Thank you. That means a lot."

"You're welcome. I'm speaking the truth. You don't need to apologize to anyone about who you are. Nobody has the right to judge you because of your background. Just like everyone else on this planet, you didn't get to choose which family you were born into. What you do have a choice about is what you've done with your life, and you've done a brilliant job."

Vanya put her arms around Nia. "Thank you," she whispered.

"You're welcome." Nia hugged Vanya and then settled back into her seat. "I get why Tendo is struggling. I didn't exactly grow up in the lap of luxury. Maybe it is a matter of his principles and not just him being resentful because he got passed over. I'm sorry it didn't work out. But big sister truth bomb?"

Vanya laughed in spite of her tears. "'Big' sister? What are you, all of three months older than I am?"

Nia smiled back. "I'm married to your big brother, so I get extra credit. Seriously, though, you need to work on yourself. You are a talented, kind, beautiful daughter of God. Be confident in that and don't let anyone make you feel ashamed of who you are."

Over the next few days, Vanya let Nia's words simmer as she settled into the new normal. Tendo didn't reach out to her, and she avoided interacting with him beyond what was strictly necessary. She never met him without Pamela or Melissa present. Though he treated her with a cold politeness which stabbed her heart, she discovered she could handle the pain of seeing him every day.

Thankfully, there was plenty to keep her mind occupied at work so she didn't have to spend hours thinking about Tendo. They had a massive Derek-shaped problem and it was up to her to sort it out. In less than three months, Tymbrian Homes was going to start a big sales push for its latest residential project. The sales department was expecting her team to deliver a collection of video testimonials from happy customers. No matter what her father said, she could not keep Derek on this project without forever damaging the company's reputation with the customers he was antagonizing.

Somebody else would need to finish the video testimonials project. But with Derek taking up so much of this quarter's budget, she'd need to find extra funds to pay for a new videography team. She arranged a meeting with the chief financial officer and convinced him to give her department a portion of the company's contingency funds.

As soon as she heard that the extra cash was approved, she punched the air and thanked God, and prayed that Eden would be available to step in once more to fix the mess Derek had left.

After rehearsing the words she would say, she picked up the phone and dialed the videographer. Her palms grew slick with sweat and her heart pounded as she waited for Eden to pick up.

"Eden Tracy."

"Hi, it's Vanya from Tymbrian Homes. You're probably surprised to hear from me."

Vanya heard a sharp intake of breath before Eden replied. "Hello. Yes, I am. What can I do for you?"

Vanya drew in a deep breath and prayed for the right words to use. "First of all, I know you might be reluctant to work with us after how we let you go last time. But I want to offer you another contract. Would you be willing to work with us again?"

There was a moment's silence on the other end of the line. "That's, um... that's quite a request. It would depend on what you want me to do and what your timeline is like."

Vanya explained what she wanted and said, "I can send you a full project brief if you're willing to take on the work."

"I can, although I'll have to move a few other projects around. If I do it, it means I'm postponing another chance to earn so I can fit you in. I can't afford to have any last-minute cancellations."

Vanya felt the sting of Eden's unspoken rebuke. "I understand. You have my word we won't pull out this time."

"Thank you."

"No, thank you. I'll get the brief sent to you immediately, and we can get the ball rolling."

Vanya ended the call. *Thank you, Lord!* Now maybe they had a chance to actually meet their deadlines.

She opened her email software and composed a message to Derek, telling him they needed him to work on a new project instead of the testimonials. She did her best to sell him on the idea of using drones to film footage of the company's country clubs. Weren't guys supposed to be excited about using electronic gadgets?

When that message was sent, the only thing left to do was inform her team. She wrote a brief message to Tendo, telling him Eden would be taking over the testimonials and asking him to supervise the project. His first task would be to send Eden the project brief.

Email was a wonderful thing. It meant she could tell Tendo work-related things without having to speak to him, see his face, or hear his voice.

A few moments later, he sent a reply as devoid of personality as hers.

Chapter Thirty

ENDO WATCHED the video montage of heartwarming images of a family sitting around the dinner table, followed by the mother placing a pile of towels inside a linen closet, and the father helping his child with homework.

The father, who a caption identified as "Jeff, 38, Surgeon," spoke to an off-screen interviewer about how quickly and smoothly their purchase had gone through when they bought a property at one of Tymbrian Homes' Surrey developments.

As the video closed, the mother's voice spoke over a perfectly framed shot of the family relaxing in their living room. "Thanks to Tymbrian, we found our perfect forever home."

Tendo looked at Eden and smiled. "Excellent. I love these."

She had been showing him the video testimonials she had produced a full week ahead of schedule. She took the laptop back from him. "Thanks. I'll upload them all to the cloud."

Tendo shook his head, still smiling. Eden and her team had been a dream to work with, especially when contrasted with the nightmare of the Derek days. He had no idea how Vanya had found the funds necessary to hire Eden again.

In the weeks since their breakup, she only doled information out to him on a need-to-know basis. But pulling Derek off the testimonials and bringing Eden back had been a brilliant move.

Derek was apparently playing with camera drones all around the

United Kingdom, taking aerial pictures over the company's country clubs. He was barely seen around the office anymore, which suited Tendo just fine. He didn't know the timeline of the country club project and had not seen any of the footage.

From what he could gather, Vanya's strategy was to have Eden and her team work on the urgent and high priority video projects, the ones which would be used during the sales campaign that was starting in just over a week.

Eden slid her folded laptop into her laptop backpack and looked at Tendo, her head tilted. "So, are you okay?"

Tendo frowned. "Of course. Why wouldn't I be?"

Eden shrugged. "Breaking up can be tough."

He froze and stared at her. "Wh-what?"

"It's none of my business, but it's pretty clear to anyone with two eyes in their head that there used to be something between you and Vanya and now there isn't. I was just asking whether you're okay."

A coldness spread through Tendo's core. He was in too much shock to formulate a denial. "How did you know?"

"I've known you how long now, five years? In all that time, I've never seen you behave the way you did around her. It was obvious watching the two of you, the way you'd look at each other and joke. And when I came back to work with you, it's been the complete opposite. Now, you repel each other like magnets turned the wrong way."

He made an effort to close his mouth, which had been hanging open. If Eden had seen all that, who else had noticed? Of course, there was Suzy, but she had a naturally

suspicious mind and enjoyed fling-
ing mud at everyone. He could have
sworn he and Vanya had kept their
relationship under wraps.

Eden raised her hands. "If you
don't want to talk about it, that's perfectly fine. I just wanted to check
that you're okay." She turned her
eyes back to her backpack and continued stowing the rest of her things.

Tendo pushed a hand through his
hair and sighed. "You're right. We
dated for a short time and broke up.
I guess it's just one of those things.
We come from completely different
worlds. What's that proverb? If a
bird and a fish fall in love, where
would they make a home?"

Eden was silent for several seconds. "Love, huh?"

Tendo's face grew warm at the realization of the word he'd chosen.
He didn't answer, and after a few
moments Eden asked, "So, you
ended it?"

"She did."

"Ouch. No wonder things are so awkward."

Tendo smiled wryly. "And I thought I was doing such a good job appearing like it was business as usual."

"Sorry to disappoint you, but I picked up on the weird vibe as soon as I came back. I'll pray for you."

"Thanks. I appreciate that."

"Do you want me to pray for you to get over her or that you'll get back together?"

Once again, Tendo stared slack-jawed at her, thrown off balance. "I... I don't know, to be honest. It wasn't my choice to break up, but maybe it would never have worked. Just pray that both of us would walk in whatever plans God has for us."

Eden smiled at him and left the room. Tendo remained sitting where he was for a long time afterward.

Seeing Vanya every day, so close and yet cut off from him, was torture. But the only way to handle it was to face the fact that it was over. He could live with the anguish of losing her. He didn't know if he could survive the slow torment of clinging to a fading hope of getting her back. Eden could pray however she wanted but for his own sanity, Tendo had given up hope.

Chapter Thirty-One

ATE ONE Friday evening several days later, Vanya glanced at the clock on her office wall. It was time to go, and she was keen to start this long weekend. Eden's customer testimonial videos had gone live, as had the other supporting material her department had been working hard to produce.

The head of the sales department was thrilled with all the new content his team could use, telling Vanya they were already getting a lot of customer interest and engagement.

Relieved at how she had resolved the video production situation, she could now focus her attention on the next pressing issue on her mind. She turned to look at her computer screen and re-read her resignation letter.

Her intention to leave her job had started as a small seed shortly after she'd split up with Tendo. She'd taken Nia's encouragement to heart, and believed she shouldn't have to feel guilty or apologetic about her background opening doors for her. But at the same time, she had a growing sense that this position rightly belonged to Tendo.

Although he had backtracked after comparing her father's imposition of Derek with her own hiring, her conscience told her he was right. Her letter recommended that Tendo ought to lead the team.

Vanya wasn't entirely sure what she was going to do after leaving Tymbrian Homes. She didn't need a job and could afford to take time off to figure out what to do next, and that was a reflection of her privilege. She was certain she didn't want to take another family job just yet. It was time to step out into the wide world on her own two feet.

She highlighted the resignation letter and was about to paste it into an email to her father when Derek came breezing into her office.

Grinning as though his arrival were long-expected and wished for, he slid into an armchair. "I took a chance that you would be here. The video series is done. I've brought them here for your perusal."

Vanya stared at him. "That's unexpected. I had no idea you were anywhere near completion."

"I like to exceed expectations. Do you want to have a look?"

She checked her watch. She could spare about half an hour before she needed to leave. If the videos were good, the sales department would be thrilled to have yet more material to use in their campaign. "I only have about thirty minutes."

"Great stuff. I'll set everything up." He got his tablet out and started the first video.

Vanya leaned forward. It was much better than she'd expected. Excellent, in fact. To a background of soaring classical music, the camera showed majestic aerial views of a country club house that had once been a stately home. The footage took in the pristine golf course set next to a lake. The video was exactly what Vanya had wanted, showcasing the club to perfection. When it was over, she looked at Derek and smiled. "That's really good."

He grinned. "Thank you. Wait till you see the one in Cornwall. That's next." He paused before starting the second video. "All by yourself here tonight? Can I interest you in joining me for dinner or a drink to celebrate the success of this project?"

She shook her head. "No, thanks. I have plans."

He made a face. "Too bad. Can I at least get you a coffee from the break room? I need one myself."

Vanya didn't want to share a drink with Derek on any terms, but she agreed in order to be polite. "Thanks. I take mine black."

"Sure thing." He smiled at her again and walked out of the office while she turned her attention back to the screen and tapped the play button.

Tendo was working late. He wanted to finalize his end-of-quarter report before going into the long weekend. Not that he had anything special to do. Before their breakup, he and Vanya had made vague plans about watching a West End musical this bank holiday weekend. He sighed. He could go hours without thinking about her, only for a random thought like that to pop up.

He reached for his coffee cup, noticing for the first time that it was empty. Should he get a refill or not? He dithered for a while before deciding to get a cup of tea instead. He walked into the break room and stopped short. Derek was there, standing in front of two mugs with steaming drinks on the counter.

Derek's head jerked up when Tendo walked in, and he shoved something into his pocket before smiling in greeting. It wasn't much of a smile. It looked more like he was baring his teeth. "Hello, Tendo. Working late today?"

Tendo stared at him. He'd never liked Derek, but something about the man made him especially uneasy right now. The hair on the back of his neck stood as he moved over to the sink with his mug. He did his best to keep his tone light. "Trying to get some things finished before the weekend, but I'll be done before long. How are you getting on with your project?"

Derek smiled again. "Great, actually. We're all done. I came to show Vanya the completed videos."

Tendo did a double take. "Completed? That's good news. Great job."

"Thank you. Vanya seems to like them a lot. She's looking them over now. I'll catch you later." He nodded at Tendo and picked up the mugs before leaving the room.

Tendo watched him go, frowning. Why was he feeling on edge? He shrugged it off and put the kettle on.

Chapter Thirty-Two

VANYA HAD watched the video of the Cornwall country club and started on the one filmed in Wales when Derek came back into her office carrying two mugs.

He placed one in front of her. "There you go. Black coffee."

"Thanks." She pulled the mug toward her. "These are all perfect so far. If the rest of them are like this, we won't need any changes made at all."

"Glad to hear it."

Vanya sipped her coffee. When she looked up, Derek's eyes were fixed on her. He turned his gaze away and motioned toward the tablet. "What do you think of Wales?"

"Fantastic. You seem to have been lucky with the weather."

"Yes, that was fortunate. You haven't come to my favorites yet: the clubs in Scotland. Have you visited them, by the way?"

She shook her head. "No, I haven't been to either of the clubs north of the border. Looking forward to seeing the pictures you got from there."

Derek remained silent while Vanya watched three more of the short videos. She passed a hand over her eyes. Drowsiness slammed into her like a wall, and it was suddenly hard to keep her eyes open. She turned to Derek. "I think I've seen enough for now." At least, she tried to say it, but her mouth wouldn't obey her brain and the words came out slurred.

Her heart began pounding. What was going on? She attempted to stand up but, like her mouth, her limbs were disconnected from her brain. The last thing she saw before everything went black was Derek's eyes glittering as he watched her.

Tendo shut down his laptop and rolled the kinks out of his shoulders. The report was done, and he was ready to go home. He hesitated for a moment, debating whether or not to take his laptop with him. No, he decided. He was going to switch off from work completely this weekend. It was time he filled up his mind with something else.

Perhaps he could scope out other potential job openings. Working around Vanya wasn't getting any easier. Since his talk with Eden, he felt even more on edge about how many more people might notice the vibes between him and his boss.

Getting another job was looking like a more and more attractive possibility. His non-compete clause limited his options, but there were still other things he could do.

Maybe he'd spend some time updating his resume and LinkedIn profile.

He stepped into the hallway and was on his way to the elevators when a crash came from Vanya's office, followed by a muffled expletive. Tendo froze in his tracks. That had been a man's voice. What was going on? The door was slightly ajar, so he pushed it open.

Vanya, her eyes closed, lay slumped on the sofa in the corner of her office. Derek knelt beside her, dabbing a dark stain on his pants leg with tissues. A mug lay shattered in pieces on the floor. Derek looked up at Tendo, his face red.

Tendo strode into the office. "What's going on?"

Derek shrugged. "She, um... She... We were having shots to celebrate my completing the promotional videos, and she had one too many."

Tendo's stomach knotted up. He gestured around the room. "I don't see any glasses. And I know Vanya doesn't drink alcohol."

The blood drained from Derek's face, but he leered as he stood up. "Is that what she told you? I've known Vanya almost all my life and, believe me, she drinks. We mixed the stuff in our coffee and I managed to spill some on myself." Derek picked up a set of keys from the table and shoved them into his pocket. "No need for you to hang around. I'll see that she gets home."

At Derek's gesture, an image flashed in Tendo's mind, of Derek putting something in his pocket when Tendo had walked in on him in the breakout room. Derek had been standing in front of the coffee mugs and he'd tucked something away as soon as he'd seen Tendo.

As the pieces fell together in Tendo's mind, white hot rage flooded his body. He clenched his fists and his breath quickened. With a supreme effort, he stopped himself from grabbing Derek by the throat.

He scanned the room. A mug sat on the table, a smudge of pink lipstick on its rim. Pulling a handkerchief out of his pocket, he picked up the mug. He turned to face Derek, speaking through gritted teeth. "What did you give her?"

Derek's face darkened. "You're out of your mind. I suggest you turn around and get out of here."

His eyes never leaving Derek's face, Tendo set the mug down. He stepped over to Vanya's desk phone. He needed to call the police. But that might take too long, and he had no idea what Derek might try to do. He pushed a button. "Is that security? I need you in Miss Klassen's office. Room 415. There's been an attempted assault and the suspect is still on the premises. Please come immediately."

Derek's eyes bulged as he stared at Tendo. "You're completely mad. What are you talking about?"

"You know exactly what I'm talking about."

Derek took a step toward Tendo. Tendo shifted his position, planting one foot slightly forward as he raised up his hands and dipped his chin. Derek hesitated, and part of Tendo wished the other man would give him an excuse to slam a fist into that smug lying mouth.

Derek, his face flushed, pivoted to the table. He grabbed his tablet and tucked it under his arm. "This is ridiculous. I'm leaving."

"You're not going anywhere unless you flatten me first."

Derek shot him a poisonous glare. He fumbled in his pocket and pulled out his cell phone, spitting his words out at Tendo. "I'll have you for false imprisonment. We'll see who the authorities believe. A close friend of the Klassen family or an upstart nobody like you."

Tendo didn't answer but held his ground, blocking Derek's path to the door. Derek unleashed a stream of filthy words but, despite his threats, he didn't make any call on his phone. Where were the security people?

Fear gnawed at the edges of Tendo's rage. He had no idea what Derek had given Vanya. She needed medical attention. If the people from security delayed much longer, he would let Derek go and focus on getting Vanya help.

The sound of footsteps behind him and the look on Derek's face told him that help had finally arrived. Two security guards rushed into the room.

Tendo turned toward them. "I think this man has spiked Miss Klassen's drink with some sort of drug. Would you please hold him and contact the police? Give them my phone number and tell them I've got the cup which I believe to have held the spiked drink. I'm going to take her to the hospital." He reached into his jacket pocket and gave one of the guards his business card.

Derek spoke up. "This is all a ridiculous misunderstanding. Do you know who I am? This man is telling the most outrageous lies, and I demand that you let me go."

The guards looked from Tendo to Derek. Tendo's pulse raced even faster. Surely they wouldn't believe Derek. Would they? Finally, one of the guards said to Tendo, "We'll take care of this, Mr. Halloran. You just make sure Miss Klassen gets to the hospital."

Tendo rushed to where Vanya still lay unmoving on the sofa. He touched her face. "Vanya?" She was unresponsive. He slipped an arm behind her shoulders and raised her up. Cradling her to his chest, feeling moisture on his cheeks but not caring who was watching, he pulled his cell phone out of his pocket and dialed the emergency services.

Chapter Thirty-Three

BY THE time Tendo finished giving his statement to the police, over three hours had gone by. Three hours of trying to keep his gut-gnawing anxiety at bay and focus his mind on passing the officers all the information they needed to investigate Vanya's attack and hopefully put Derek away.

When he signed his statement and left the station, one thought filled his mind: finding out how she was. It was past midnight, but he hailed a black cab to take him back to the emergency room where he had last seen Vanya being wheeled away.

He had no idea whether he would be allowed to see her or learn any news about her current condition, but he couldn't bear to be anywhere else. He took a ticket from the queuing system and sat to wait, praying silently.

His number beeped on the screen and he hurried to the counter. A nurse with iron gray hair and a brisk air looked up at him. "Hello. Can you describe what happened and your symptoms?"

Tendo shook his head. "Sorry, it's not me. I'm fine. I'm here to inquire about a patient I brought in earlier this evening, almost four hours ago."

She pinned him with a steely glare. "This desk is for dealing with acutely ill patients, not for taking inquiries."

Tendo laid his hands flat on the counter. "I know, and I'm sorry. I'm just desperate to know how she is. Someone gave her some sort of date rape drug and she passed out. I want to know whether she'll be okay."

The nurse stared at his face, and her eyes softened. "What's her name?"

"Vanya Klassen."

"Do you know her date of birth and address?"

Tendo knew Vanya's birthday, but he had to check his phone for her address. When he gave the nurse the information, she nodded. "She's in room 4C. Follow the yellow line down the hall and to your right."

"Thank you!"

He wanted to run down the hall, but restrained himself to a brisk walk. He found room 4C and pushed the door open. His eyes swept the large room. It was partitioned with screens, a bed in each makeshift cubicle. At the far corner closest to the window, a fair-haired man sat in a chair next to a bed. He looked so much like a masculine version of Vanya that Tendo knew this must be one of her brothers.

He walked up to the man, who looked up at him. Tendo glanced at the bed where Vanya lay sleeping, or unconscious. He turned back to her brother and held out his hand.

"Hello. My name is Tendo Halloran, and I work with Vanya. I came in with her earlier and wanted to make sure she's okay."

Recognition lighted up the man's eyes, and he stood, taking Tendo's hand. "Hi. I'm her brother, Magnus. You brought her in? Can you tell me what happened? The police were here, but they weren't able to give me much information."

Tendo nodded. "Absolutely. How is she?"

They both turned to look at Vanya. Magnus said, "The doctor seems to think she'll be okay. They did a preliminary test that showed she has a date rape drug, GHB, in her system." He turned to face Tendo. "Do you know how that happened?"

Tendo clenched his fists. Heat washed over his body. He'd suspected it, but hearing confirmation of what Derek had done filled him with white hot rage. He gritted his teeth until his jaw hurt and made an effort to take several slow deep breaths. The police were handling this. More importantly, God was in control. He looked up. Magnus was watching him intently.

Tendo said, "I promised to tell you what happened. Maybe we can find somewhere to talk?"

Magnus nodded and threw another glance at Vanya. "Sure. They'll be moving her to a private room soon, and I want to be here when they do that. If we can sit outside in the hallway, I won't miss the nurses if they come."

They found a seating area a short way down the hall, near a bank of vending machines. Tendo began to speak as soon as they sat down. "I'll tell you everything I know. My office is a few doors away from Vanya's, and we use the same break room to get coffee and tea and so on. I'd gone to get a cup of tea, and I saw a man who we've been working with, Derek Coleman-Baines."

Magnus's jaw tightened, but he didn't interrupt. Tendo continued. "He seemed surprised to see me and a bit edgy, and I thought I saw him hiding something in his pocket. He had two cups of coffee with him. I put it out of my mind and carried on with what I was doing. When I was on my way out, I was just outside Vanya's office when I heard something falling and a man's voice swearing."

The back of Tendo's throat ached as moisture sprang to his eyes. "I went in and found Derek kneeling next to Vanya. She was completely out of it on the sofa. He told a bare-faced lie about how Vanya had been drinking shots, and that's when I started joining all the dots. I stopped him from leaving and called security and as soon as they took charge of Derek, I called an ambulance for Vanya and rode here with her. The police were quick to come to the hospital and I went to the station with them to give a full statement. I came back here as soon as I was finished."

Magnus clenched and unclenched his fists. "Derek Coleman-Baines. I knew he was a scumbag, but I never thought he'd do something like this." He turned his eyes to Tendo. "Thank God you were there. If you hadn't been—" he broke off, and Tendo understood. Giving voice to what Derek might have done was too painful for him as well.

"Thank God," Tendo repeated. He slumped back into his chair as the emotional and physical strain of the day rushed upon him like a tidal wave. He didn't have an excuse or a right to stay in the hospital now that Vanya's family were here. He looked at Magnus. "Would you give me an update in the morning about how she's doing?"

"Of course. Give me your number." Magnus pulled his phone out and unlocked the screen.

Tendo hesitated a moment. "I ought to tell you that Vanya and I dated briefly until a few weeks ago when she ended things. I probably don't have a right to any info, but I'd like to know how she's getting on."

Magnus stared at him. "Wait... you're that guy? My wife told me something about what happened." He crossed his arms and sized Tendo up. After what felt like an eternity to Tendo, Magnus said, "I won't pry into why it didn't work out, and I'd normally have a major bone to pick with any guy who broke my little sister's heart. But after what you did today, we all owe you. I think you're entitled to know how she's doing. What's your number?"

Tendo dictated his number and Magnus tapped it into his phone. Magnus looked up at him. "Thanks. I'll send you a text message so you can store my number as well." He stood up. "I'd better go back to Vanya now. Thanks once again."

Tendo nodded. "I'll be praying." Magnus extended his hand and Tendo grasped it. They shook hands in silence and Tendo watched as Magnus walked down the hallway and went back into Vanya's room. Tendo headed slowly to the exit, completely spent. There was nothing more he could do but pray.

Chapter Thirty-Four

ANYA RETCHED so violently she thought her insides were going to come out. A cool hand rested on her forehead and she felt herself being pushed gently back onto soft pillows. Where was she? She attempted to open her eyelids, but gave up. The light was too piercing. She opened her mouth to speak, but another wave of nausea hit.

Someone was wiping her mouth with something cool and wet. "Thank you," Vanya mumbled before she sank back into sleep.

She woke up with a sharp jolt and stared around her. A hospital room? She was trying to make sense of this when someone touched her hand. "You're awake. Thank God!"

Vanya turned her head to the sound of the voice. Nia was staring at her, eyes moist. Nia? What was she doing here? For that matter, what was she herself doing here? She tried to think, but the images in her mind were fragmented, like a jumbled up and broken film reel. She was sitting at her desk about to go home. Then she was watching videos on a tablet. Derek was smiling at her. She closed her eyes, a searing pain knifing her brain.

Something cool was pressed against her forehead. She opened her eyes again. Nia was holding a damp cloth to her face. Vanya smiled. "Thank you." Her voice was a harsh croak. "What happened? Did I have an accident?"

Nia turned her head to look at someone and Vanya realized for the first time that her brother Magnus was also in the room. He said, "Hi, little sister. A police officer is on the way. They wanted you to tell them what you remember as soon as you wake up."

Police officer? Vanya tried to sit up but gave up after the pounding in her head intensified. Why did the police want to speak to her? Nia squeezed her hand. "I'll get you a drink of water."

Vanya sipped the water gratefully. It soothed her parched throat. She closed her eyes again and must have fallen asleep because she woke up to Nia gently touching her shoulder. Vanya looked up to see a uniformed police officer sitting in the chair.

The woman introduced herself as police constable Julie Grant. "I'm sorry to bother you, and I won't take up much of your time, but it's important I get a statement from you. Can you tell me everything you remember from last night?"

Vanya frowned. "Why? What happened?"

"I'll tell you in a moment, but it's very important that you tell us exactly what you remember so we don't influence your memories."

Vanya stared at the police officer. None of this made any sense. "I remember being in my office. I was about to finish work. I was planning on visiting my brother but I didn't go. I had to stay for something." She closed her eyes and rubbed her temples. "I think I was watching something. Not a movie." Her voice trailed off.

"You're doing great, Vanya," PC Grant said. "It might help to close your eyes and relax."

Vanya obeyed and lay back. More images came. "I think I was watching videos on a tablet. It wasn't my tablet." She frowned. "It was Derek's. He'd completed his work early and was showing me what he'd done."

She was silent for a long moment. PC Grant spoke. "Can you remember having anything to drink?"

Vanya opened her eyes. "I had some coffee. Derek made me some coffee." Her breath caught as a new image flashed into her mind of Derek watching her, his eyes tracking her like a snake stalking a mouse. Her heart began racing as a thought too hideous for words took shape. "Did he—" Her throat tightened up and she couldn't finish the sentence. Nia grabbed her hand.

PC Grant asked, "Is that all you remember?"

Vanya gasped for breath. "Yes. Except his face. He was watching me with this look on his face." She shuddered.

"You've done a brilliant job, Vanya. I won't trouble you anymore." The police officer closed her notebook. "I can tell you, though, that we are investigating a very serious crime. The hospital has confirmed that you have a substance called GHB in your body. It was also found in a cup that contained a small amount of coffee. The cup has gone for further testing, which we believe will confirm you were in contact with it. We also have a witness who found you unconscious in your office with the individual you named also present."

Vanya's mouth went dry. PC Grant continued, "If it will put your mind at rest, we believe the witness arrived soon after you lost consciousness. As far as we can tell, there was no physical or sexual assault." She smiled. "It may not feel like it, but you're a very lucky woman, Vanya."

"Who was the witness?"

PC Grant consulted her notes. "A colleague of yours. Tendo Halloran. He arranged for you to come to the hospital."

Vanya's mind reeled. Tendo had been there? "You think Derek put the GHB into my drink?"

"The evidence strongly suggests that. Derek is in custody now, pending further inquiries."

Vanya felt moisture on her face and realized tears were trickling down. Derek had spiked her drink, possibly planning to rape her, and Tendo had stopped him. She put her hand over her mouth and gasped. "I'm going to be sick."

Nia was ready with an emesis basin as Vanya retched. She lay back, trembling, as Nia went into the bathroom.

PC Grant stood up. "I'll let you get some rest. I'll be back later to take a formal statement from you. Goodbye." She nodded at Magnus and left the room.

Magnus said, "Tendo stopped by here after he gave his statement to the police. He wanted to find out how you were, and he asked me to update him this morning. Are you okay with me letting him know you're awake and doing fine?"

Vanya swallowed. Tendo had come back to check on her? Warmth spread inside her. Didn't that mean that despite how things had ended between them, she still mattered to him? Or at least she mattered enough for him to check up on her? On top of everything else she already felt for him, now she could add "rescuer". But she was supposed to be moving on and putting their relationship in the past.

She was grateful God had sent somebody to save her. But did it have to be Tendo? He was already embedded so deep in her heart she didn't know how to kick him out. And now she owed him for protecting her.

Magnus was looking at her. She nodded. "Yes, that's fine." She watched as Magnus tapped on his phone. "Tell him—"

Magnus glanced up at her. "Tell him what?"

She hesitated for a long moment, then said. "Nothing. Just let him know I'm fine."

Tendo was having a late breakfast when his phone pinged. His eyes filled up as they devoured the message from Magnus. Vanya was okay. *Thank you, Lord.* He'd crashed from sheer exhaustion last night, but since he'd woken up, she had been on his mind. He'd been checking his phone what felt like every five minutes for any word about how she was doing.

He texted back. **Thanks for letting me know. I'll keep praying.**

Praying. He'd done little else every waking minute. Praying for

Vanya, for the police to do a thorough investigation and pin Derek for what he'd done.

Throughout the emotional upheaval of the past hours, one thing had become as clear as day to Tendo.

He loved Vanya.

Seeing her in danger, knowing how close Derek had been to violating her, he'd known that her wellbeing was the most important thing in his life. With that realization came the painful reality that it was probably too late to do anything about it. Their relationship was over. He'd had his chance and blown it, and he couldn't see a way back.

He couldn't push her to think about him now, not when she was trying to get over this ugly incident with Derek. He'd have to be satisfied with watching her from afar, being close enough to see her, but never able to be in her life again.

Chapter Thirty-Five

VANYA'S BROTHERS and their wives tussled over who should take her home with them. It soothed her battered spirit to know how much they all wanted her. In the end, she decided to go with Magnus and Nia.

Now, although she'd been settled in a guest bedroom and left with orders to rest, she was finding it impossible to go to sleep. Nausea and headaches still plagued her.

The doctors had warned her she would probably never fully regain any recollection of what Derek had said or done after drugging her, but she couldn't help trying to dredge her mind for any fragments of memory.

The police officer had assured her Derek hadn't had the chance to do anything beyond knocking her out. That was a huge relief. She wished she could remember Tendo coming to help her.

There was a soft knock on her door.

"Come in." She brushed a tear away. There was no reason to be upset. She was fine. Derek hadn't hurt her.

Her parents stepped into the room. Her mother rushed forward and pulled Vanya into a hug. Karl, never one to show affection, only patted her hand.

Jessica dabbed at her eyes with a tissue. "We came straight from the airport. Are you okay?"

"I'm fine. Just tired and nauseous."

"And Magnus says the police have arrested Derek. I can't believe it. What happened?"

Karl looked at his wife. "Let's not trouble her, Jessica. She's been through enough. She needs to rest."

Jessica fussed over Vanya's pillows and announced she was going to spend some time with her grandson. Vanya suppressed a wry smile. Her mother was no Florence Nightingale. Sitting beside a sickbed was not one of Jessica's strong points.

Karl watched her go and turned back to Vanya. She'd never known him to be at a loss for words before, but he clenched his fists and cleared his throat several times before he spoke. "I... I'm very sorry to hear about all this, Vanya. And I feel responsible because I insisted you work with that piece of filth. I'll do everything I can to ensure he does not get away with this."

He took hold of Vanya's hand and squeezed it.

Vanya's throat was tight. "Thank you."

"Don't worry about work. Take as much time off as you need. Your deputy will fill in until you're ready to come back."

He stood to leave, but she said, "Why not make it permanent?"

Karl sat down again, staring at her. "Make what permanent?"

"I was thinking about stepping aside even before... before all this happened. I've even written my resignation letter."

He frowned. "Aren't you happy working at Tymbrian Homes? Your department has been doing exceptional work."

"I've enjoyed working there, and we've got a wonderful team. But Tendo is the real driving force behind the department's success. He can more than fill my shoes."

Karl rubbed his chin. "Let's not make any hasty decisions. You've been through a lot. We'll discuss this when you've had more time to process everything."

"It's not a hasty decision. It's been on my mind for a while. I was planning on talking to you about it when you returned from your vacation."

Karl studied her face for a long while. "Okay, then, if you're sure."

A few days later, Tendo stood outside Karl Klassen's office in response to a summons. He took a few deep breaths to calm his nerves, and knocked.

"Come in."

Tendo stepped inside. He'd never been here before, but he barely registered the plush leather, modern art pieces, and teak paneling. His eyes were on Karl. The older man stood behind his desk and extended his hand. Tendo took it, hoping his own wasn't clammy.

Karl motioned toward a chair. "Please have a seat, Tendo. Can I offer you a drink?"

Tendo sat, holding himself upright. "No, thank you."

Karl sat down and rested his elbows on his desk, surveying Tendo over steepled fingers. Finally, he said, "I asked you here for two reasons. First of all, I want to thank you for what you did last week. Your intervention prevented a despicable criminal act from being many times worse. So, thank you."

Tendo swallowed. "You're welcome. I only wish I could have been there even earlier."

"So do I." Tendo was surprised by the husky tone of Karl's voice. The older man cleared his throat and stared at his hands for a moment. He looked up again, his face composed.

"The second reason I want to speak with you is about your place in this company. Since you began working here, you've distinguished yourself in every role you've been given. Now, since the position has fallen vacant, I wanted to personally ask you to head the brand publishing department. I'm confident you have everything it takes to continue the excellent work this department has already started."

Tendo stared at him, aware of what he was being offered, but fixated on one word. "Fallen vacant? Is Vanya not returning to work?"

Karl shook his head. "She gave me her resignation a few days ago. Given the circumstances, I waived the usual notice period. She recommended you very highly for the role and said she had been planning on stepping down even before the incident with Derek. You've already been filling in for her while she's been away, so this would just make it official."

Tendo rubbed his knuckles. This was what he had always wanted and worked so hard for. The ninety-hour work weeks with no social life, countless ages spent studying and learning, it had all been about coming to this point, the pinnacle of his profession.

It meant financial security for himself and being able to ensure his mother could retire with dignity and live in a decent neighborhood where people didn't throw bricks through her window and shove refuse in her letter box.

He had arrived. Except this wasn't where he wanted to be anymore. Now that he had the huge salary, the prestige, within his grasp, it had lost its luster. It meant nothing to him without somebody to share it with, without Vanya.

The time he and Vanya had been together had given him a glimpse into what life could be like when he walked side by side with a kind, smart, godly, beautiful woman. She had filled his life with light and laughter. And now she was going. He might never see her again.

Karl stared at him, clearly waiting for an answer. Tendo opened his mouth to speak, but no sound came out.

Karl's mouth tipped up in a smile. "I understand. You want to see the contract. Smart young man. I'll get it drawn up so you can have a look at it first." He rose and held his hand out again. "Thank you once more, and I hope we'll speak soon."

Tendo thanked him and left.

Chapter Thirty-Six

VANYA'S HAND trembled as it closed round the handle of her office door. *You can do this. It's just a room. Four walls, a roof and a door. Just an empty room.* She looked back over her shoulder at Nia. "Thanks for giving up your Saturday morning to come here with me."

Nia smiled. "You're more than welcome."

Vanya opened the door and stepped inside. Sunlight filtered through the vertical blinds onto her bow-fronted desk. Her large-screen monitor, mouse, and keyboard sat there as always. So much had happened in this office. This is where she met Tendo for the first time and worked with him every day. She'd sat behind that desk and watched that awful YouTube video on that computer, and he'd been there to comfort her. And this was where she'd realized she and Tendo had no future.

She'd been afraid of coming here because she had thought it would bring back memories of Derek's assault. Instead, the room was full of ghosts of her failed relationship with Tendo.

Her eyes moistened and she dashed a tear away with her sleeve. Nia touched her shoulder. "If being here is too much for you, you can go and I'll pack up your things. I know this place might be triggering."

Vanya shook her head. "No, it's not that. I'm fine. Really. Let's get on with it." She and Nia each had a cardboard storage box, and Vanya placed hers on her desk.

Nia looked around. "Tell me where to start."

"You can begin with the middle and bottom drawers. Those have my personal stationery. And there's also three of those potted plants on the windowsill. The aloe, cactus, and peace lily are mine. I'll sort through the bookshelf."

"Got it."

Nia opened the first drawer while Vanya slid open the glass-fronted bookshelf. She ran her finger along the books' spines, pulling out the ones she'd bought for herself and wanted to keep. They worked in silence for several minutes. Vanya's heart leapt when someone knocked on the door. She glanced up to see Tendo standing there.

Her heart seemed to have forgotten how to beat, then it thudded back into action, drumming a crazy rhythm. Nia looked at Vanya, then turned around toward the door.

Tendo stepped forward, his eyes fixed on Vanya. "I thought I heard someone in here. I didn't know it would be you."

"I came to get my things." She brushed a strand of hair off her face. "What are you doing here on a Saturday?"

"I took some work home, then realized I'd forgotten to transfer the files I needed to the cloud, so I had to come back and copy them." He turned toward Nia, as though he'd just seen her. "I'm sorry— I'm Tendo."

Nia's eyebrows flew up. "Ah, so you're Tendo. *Gyebale ko, ssebo.*"

His mouth fell open. "*Gyebale ko, nnyabo.*"

"*Oli otya, ssebo?*"

"*Gyendi, nnyabo.*" He laughed and raised his hands. "And that's where my Luganda ends."

Nia smiled. "I'll let you off the hook. That's not bad at all. I'm

Vanya's sister-in-law. She told me she worked with someone whose mother came from Uganda. I'm from there, too."

"That explains a lot. Nice to meet you."

"Nice to meet you, too. And thank you for what you did for Vanya."

Tendo inclined his head and turned toward Vanya. "Do you have a couple of minutes? I'd like to talk, if you're not in a hurry."

"I've got a bit of time, if it's okay with Nia." She turned to look at her sister-in-law.

Nia said, "Fine by me. I'll just take this box down to the car." She leaned close to Vanya and whispered in her ear. "And maybe I'll kill some time at the Starbucks I saw across the street. Text me when you need me."

Heat flushed Vanya's face as Nia turned toward Tendo. "See you later."

Tendo stepped aside to let her go past, then looked at Vanya again. "I'm so glad to see you on your feet. Are you okay?"

She nodded. "I'm fine. I was sick as a dog for a while, but all better now. I... I haven't even thanked you properly yet. If you hadn't been there—" She broke off, a tremor in her voice.

"No need to thank me. You might as well thank me for breathing or for blinking."

She caught an undercurrent in his tone that made her stomach turn somersaults.

He gestured with his hand. "I guess this place has a lot of bad memories. I don't blame you for wanting to go without saying good-bye."

"The memories aren't all bad. I thought it would be easier if I just slipped away. But you're right. I should have said bye to... to the team."

"We'll all miss you. You're an amazing manager."

"Am I?" She stared at him. "I don't want you saying things just to be kind."

"Yes, you are. You're one of the best managers I've ever worked with. You're sharp as a whip and a big picture thinker. You have a way with people I wish I could learn. All these guys on our team? They work as hard as they do because you make them want to do their best. They're all about 'What will Vanya think about this?' and 'Vanya said we should try it this way.'"

She blinked back tears. "Really? Thank you."

"Yes, really. So, if you're going, don't go because you think you're not good enough for this job. I'm sorry I ever made you think that. When we had that fight over Derek and his actors, I said some dumb things I've regretted ever since."

"A lot of what you said was true. All of it, actually. And the job should be yours. What happened wasn't fair."

"No, I wasn't entitled to that job. I did want to run the department and was disappointed when I didn't get the role. But Tymbrian Homes is your father's company to run as he chooses. I might have my opinions about his management style, but I don't have a right to any position here. And I should never have let my frustration about your father and Derek spill over into my relationship with you. Can you forgive me for that?"

She nodded, unable to answer because of the aching lump in the back of her throat.

He squeezed his eyes shut and bowed his head. "Thank you. I'm sorry for hurting you."

"I was only hurt because you poked a particularly sore spot about whether I deserved my job or not." She smiled weakly. "Nia calls it impostor syndrome, and it's something I know I need to work on."

Tendo slapped his forehead with his palm. "Of course! I'm such an idiot. And with all that happened with that woman and the YouTube video." He groaned and pushed his hand into his hair. "I should have understood that. Vanya, I'm so sorry."

"It's okay. It's my own hypersensitivity, and I have to get over it."

"No, it's not okay." He stepped closer to her and she had to tilt her head upward to look at his face. "You were my girlfriend. I ought to have realized how much it would hurt you when I implied that your father had imposed you on this team."

"I'm not completely blameless. I could have agreed to talk things through."

"But why would you have wanted to talk anything through with a numskull like me?" he asked.

She laughed, but stopped when she saw that his expression was serious and there was a sheen of moisture in his eyes. His voice was husky. "Is it too late for me? Did I completely kill my chance with you?"

She shook her head. "No."

His fingers brushed against hers, and he wrapped her in his arms. She melted into him, and her body trembled as she cried softly, creating a spreading damp patch on his chest. They stood holding each other for a long time.

Finally, he stepped back and kissed her forehead. His thumbs gently stroked away the tears on her cheeks. "I love you, Vanya. But I don't want to put any pressure on you. I understand that maybe you're not there yet. You've been through a lot of ugly stuff lately. I'm not expecting you to feel the same way about me. I just wanted to tell you what you mean to me. I'm not going anywhere, and I'll try my hardest not to push you into anything you're not ready for."

Her heart swelled with a joy so deep that it felt more like pain. She smiled up at him through her tears. "I love you, too."

His eyes lit up and he threw his head back and whooped. She giggled and covered her ears as his voice bounced off the walls of the office. "You know, Tendo, you have a way with words. Did you ever consider a career in content marketing?"

He laughed until she stood on her tiptoes and pulled his face toward hers, stopping his laughter with a gentle kiss.

Chapter Thirty-Seven

SIX MONTHS LATER

TENDO SMILED as he came to the last page of his department's quarterly evaluation report. His team had smashed all six of their goals. A year after the brand publishing team had been pulled together, they had more than proved their worth to the company. It would be a pleasure to share these results with the board of directors when they met next week.

More than his professional success, though, Tendo was grateful to God for the amazing woman who lit up his life. Since she had left Tymbrian Homes, Vanya had started a course in child psychology.

Their relationship had flourished and deepened. Away from the pressures of the workplace and the scrutiny of their colleagues, they'd had space and time to grow closer.

Tendo knew beyond any doubt this was the woman with whom he wanted to spend the rest of his life. He missed having her here, but knew it was for the best. He'd show her a copy of this report when he saw her tonight. She'd be delighted at how much her old team had achieved.

The one cloud that had been hanging over them was Derek's trial. Tendo had been worried about Vanya having to face her attacker in court. But two weeks ago, in the face of the overwhelming evidence against him, Derek had pleaded guilty to administering a substance with intent, and was sentenced to one year's imprisonment. With that ugly episode behind them, Tendo was looking forward to what the future held.

Tendo's intercom buzzed and he picked up his phone extension. A cool crisp voice spoke into his ear. "Mr. Halloran? This is Mr. Klassen's executive secretary. Mr. Klassen would like to see you in his office immediately, please."

Tendo's eyebrows flew up. "Immediately? Okay, I'll be right over."

Tendo stood up from his desk. What could Karl want with him? He headed out to the hallway and for the bank of elevators. Karl's executive suite was on the upper floors. An elevator door opened and Suzy stepped out. She shot Tendo a look and her lips curved in a smile, but she walked off down the hallway without saying anything.

Karl's secretary ushered Tendo straight through, and he stepped into the office. The last time he'd been here was the day Karl had summoned him to offer him the promotion and thank him for rescuing Vanya. The older man had been full of gratitude and compliments that day.

But as Karl turned around from the floor-to-ceiling windows, he fixed Tendo with an icy glare. Tendo felt a prickle of unease. Whatever he'd been summoned for, it didn't appear that Karl was in a good mood.

Karl spoke in hard, clipped tones. "What's going on between you and my daughter?"

Tendo blinked in surprise. At Vanya's insistence, they had kept their relationship away from her parents. Although her brothers knew that they were dating, she said it would be better to wait to inform her parents, especially since Tendo worked for her father. To Tendo's surprise, her brothers had agreed, advising them to wait on informing

Karl and Jessica until the young couple had firm plans for the future.

Tendo did indeed have firm plans. Through some clandestine communication with her sister-in-law Nia, he'd found out Vanya's ring size. A platinum ring set with three large round diamonds had sat in his desk drawer at home for the last two weeks. He intended to propose to Vanya this weekend. They had plans to visit the beach where she'd first shown him the sea, and he thought that would be the perfect place to ask her to be his wife.

But this wasn't how he'd planned on telling his future father-in-law. He suddenly recalled Suzy's face when he'd passed her at the elevators. Had she been here spreading trouble? Karl's gray eyes drilled into him, waiting for an answer.

Tendo said, "Your daughter and I are in a relationship. I love her."

Karl scowled. "So, it is true. Let me assure you, young man, you can forget whatever designs you have on furthering your career or feathering your nest through Vanya."

Heat flashed through Tendo, but he kept his voice even. "I don't have any such designs."

"Oh, really?" Karl crossed his arms. "You mean to tell me you have no interest in her trust fund or in what being involved with her might do for your position in my company? I've always had you pegged as a man of ambition, someone who was on the make. But I'll tell you right now you will not touch a single penny of her money. If she insists on tying her future with yours, I'll make sure it's with a prenuptial agreement."

Tendo's muscles tensed and his heart pounded. Rage flooded his body. He looked down at the carpet for a moment, taking several slow breaths. Words his stepfather had spoken to him came back to his mind. *Listen to me, son, and listen well. Nobody can take your dignity away unless you surrender it to them.* Karl could throw whatever insults he wanted, but Tendo could choose how to react.

He raised his gaze back to meet Karl's. "I'm not interested in Vanya's money. I can manage just fine without it."

"And what if I terminate you right now? How do you think you'll manage? You're not getting any special treatment from me."

Tendo clenched his fists. "That's your prerogative. I don't expect any special favors from you."

A vein pulsed on Karl's temple, and he stared at Tendo. Tendo held his gaze, keeping his face impassive. Karl raised his hand in a dismissive gesture and snorted, "Get out."

His heart pounding, Tendo turned and left the room.

A few minutes later, as he walked back into his office, Tendo's phone rang. It was Vanya. He sent a quick prayer heavenward, then took a deep breath and answered.

"Is everything okay?" she asked. "My father just called me, ranting about you. Did you tell him about us?"

Tendo sighed. "He already knew. I just confirmed it."

"What did he say?" Concern edged her voice.

"Let's just say he didn't roll out the welcome mat. But I don't think we ought to have this conversation over the phone. I'll meet you straight after work and we can talk about it."

She came to his apartment later that evening. Seeing her was the highlight of his day. But as he pulled her into his arms, he could feel the tension in her body. She sat next to him on the sofa and looked into his face, gripping his hand so hard it hurt. "What did Dad say to you?"

Tendo had mulled over how much detail to give her. He'd decided to stick to the bare facts. "He suspects I'm after your money and he assured me that I'll not get a penny of it."

Vanya's face grew flushed. "He did what?"

"He also threatened to fire me."

Her eyes widened and her nostrils flared, then she punched a cushion. She jumped up and paced back and forth in front of the sofa. "I knew he might react like this. He went off the deep end with my eldest brother when Ragnar was dating someone who Dad thought was after his money. That's why I didn't want us to tell him just yet."

"I guess it came as a shock to him. Maybe he'll calm down when he's had a chance to think. In the meantime, perhaps it's time I polished up my resume."

He'd meant it as a joke, but Vanya froze, then turned slowly around to face him, her face suddenly pale. She looked at him, worry creasing a line between her eyebrows. "I'm so sorry, Tendo. You've worked so hard to get where you are, and you might lose it all just because my dad is being so unreasonable. What are we going to do?"

He stood and stepped closer to her, wrapping his arms around her. She leaned against his chest, and he pressed his lips against the top of her head. His heart swelled with love for her. She brought so much sweetness and delight into his life. Lose his job? That didn't matter. He could start again somewhere else. He wasn't afraid of hard work; that's what he'd done all his life. What he didn't want to lose was Vanya. But he had no idea what sort of pressure Karl might put on her, what being with him might cost her.

He kissed the top of her head again, then took a step back, his hands sliding to her shoulders. "I couldn't care less what Karl does to *me*. Losing my job means nothing. I can get another one. But I'm concerned about you and what you might lose by being with me."

He pulled a small velvet box out of his pocket and held it in front of her. Her hands flew up to cover her mouth, and tears filled her eyes.

Tendo smiled, despite the tears that misted up his own eyes. He opened the box and the diamond ring sparkled in the evening light. "I want you to be my wife. For myself, I don't care if I have to start my career all over again. But I don't know what I might be asking you to give up if you decide to marry me."

She looked into his face, her eyes glowing with a radiance worth more to him than all the jewels in the world. "What would I give up? A trust fund? A share of my father's money? You're the first person who looked at me, really looked at me, and loved me for who I am. And you're the most amazing man I've ever met. Your heart, your grit, your inner strength... Sometimes I can't believe how lucky I am that you want me. Give me that ring before you change your mind!"

He slid the ring onto her finger. Cupping her lovely face in his hands, he kissed away the tears on her cheeks and pressed his lips to hers. Karl, Suzy, and all their ill will could do nothing to sour the love he had for this woman.

He gathered her in his arms, holding her tightly against his heart. She had chosen him. "I love you, Vanya. I want to spend the rest of my life showing you how precious you are. I know we'll be fine."

Epilogue

EDEN TRACY sighed, blown away all over again by the beauty that surrounded her. Tendo and Vanya had chosen to have their wedding at a 150-year-old fort on the coast of Cornwall. With its stunning grounds and views over impossibly blue water, Eden knew straight away that the place would photograph like a dream. It was worth the six-hour drive to get here.

The day they'd asked her to be their wedding videographer, Vanya had told Eden they'd chosen a beachside venue because the sea was special to her and Tendo. The couple had exchanged a smiling, doe-eyed glance, and Eden didn't pry any further. People in love had inside jokes that outsiders could never fully share. Eden had seen enough besotted couples to know that.

They were getting married only ten weeks after Tendo had proposed, and needed to arrange everything in a hurry. Eden had been happy to scramble together a team to handle the video and photography for the day.

As Eden looked around the hall where the ceremony would take place, it was impossible to tell that it had all been arranged so quickly. The fort, which had long since stopped guarding Britain's coast against invasion from Europe, was now a specialized wedding venue with an in-house events organizer who'd taken the planning in hand.

Fairy lights, extravagant flowers, and cream chiffon draping gave the hall an otherworldly beauty.

Eden was thrilled for Tendo, whom she and their other friends nicknamed "The Monk," due to his nonexistent dating life and single-minded focus on work. She'd never have imagined that he would be getting married before she did.

A few years ago, she'd been close to heading down the aisle. She sighed again, inwardly this time. It was for the best, though. No need to be sad. She'd dodged a bullet.

Her videography team knew exactly what they were doing, so Eden didn't have much to do during the ceremony. When it was over, she'd use a hand-held camera to get more footage and record vox-pop style messages for the couple from their guests. Her clients often told her this was their favorite part of the wedding videos she made.

For now, she could relax, enjoy the atmosphere, and watch her friends step into their happily-ever-after

When Vanya appeared at the top of the aisle, there was a collective gasp as every eye turned toward the bride. Wearing an ethereal creation of tulle and lace, she floated down the aisle on her eldest brother Ragnar's arm.

While all eyes were on Vanya, Eden glanced at Tendo. Her heart squeezed at the raw emotion on his face as he gazed at his bride. She wondered whether anyone would ever look at her that way. But if The Monk could stumble into true love when he wasn't looking for it, perhaps there was hope for her, too.

Ragnar handed his sister to her groom and the ceremony began.

The couple exchanged their vows and Tendo serenaded his bride with a heart-piercing rendition of Richard Marx's *Now and Forever*. His adoration was almost tangible as his rich voice filled the hall. Vanya's face was aglow even through her tears, and there was hardly a dry eye in the room.

Pamela, her hair a plume of rich magenta, squeezed Eden's arm and whispered, "I had no idea he could sing! I would completely melt and you'd have to scrape me off the ground if my man sang for me like that."

Eden chuckled. "Only a heart of stone could fail to be moved by all this today. It's beautiful."

"Uh, speaking of hearts of stone. Look."

Eden turned toward where Pamela was pointing. Karl Klassen stood at the back of the room, next to a glamorous blond woman in an exquisitely tailored dress and matching hat.

Eden's heart beat faster. This was a shocker. At the rehearsal dinner yesterday, Vanya had said her parents weren't coming. Eden hadn't wanted to press for more details. Pamela had already told her that the word around the office was Tendo had fallen out of favor with the big boss.

"Karl won't fire him, though, because Tendo's too good at what he does," Pamela had said.

Eden leaned over to Pamela and whispered. "If they're showing up, maybe that means there'll be some mending of fences." Her conscience twinged even as she spoke. It was hypocritical of her to talk about fixing relationships with parents, considering the state of things between her and her own mom and dad.

She pushed the thought out of her mind. That was an entirely different scenario. There were very good reasons why she kept her parents on the fringes of her life.

Eden turned her attention back to the front of the hall, where the wedding celebrant was making his big pronouncement. "Now, by the power vested in me, I declare you man and wife. Tendo, you may kiss your bride."

The guests erupted into applause as the couple kissed. Eden stole a glance at Vanya's parents. Her mother dabbed her eyes with a tissue while Karl sat stone-faced, his arms crossed. Eden didn't think Vanya and Tendo had seen them yet.

Music filled the hall and the guests stood up. The couple walked down the aisle, followed by the bridesmaids and groomsmen.

Eden picked up her handheld camera and turned to Pamela. "I'll catch you later. I need to get some footage with this." She moved toward the back of the hall and held up her camera.

Vanya and Tendo made their way along the aisle, their fingers interlaced, smiling radiantly at their guests. As they got to the back rows, Vanya's eyes widened. Tendo, who'd been watching her face, followed her gaze and saw Mr. and Mrs. Klassen.

Eden's camera captured Vanya as she rushed toward her mother. The two women embraced. They stepped back, wiping tears from their eyes. Vanya turned to face her father. He leaned forward and said something in her ear, his hand resting on her arm.

Vanya, her face radiant, stepped back to her husband's side, threading her fingers with his. Tendo and Karl's eyes met. Tendo inclined his head and Karl stared at him for a moment before giving a curt nod and turning away.

Eden wasn't sure whether she should include this particular bit of footage in the final video package. Karl may not be over the moon by his daughter's marriage, but at least he'd come. That had to mean something.

She turned her camera back to the couple. Tendo, the Monk no more, and his wife exchanged a look and burst into spontaneous laughter. Eden smiled as well. She was sure they'd be just fine.

Read Eden's story in Hidden In Her Heart, coming to your favorite online book retailer in March 2021.

Hidden in Her Heart
Color-Blind Love
Book Four

When she needed him most, he proposed to someone else. Can she risk putting her heart on the line again?

Eden grew up in front of the camera with fame-hungry parents who exposed every corner of their family's life to a string of reality TV shows. Her only refuge was her best friend Noah. He was the anchor who kept her grounded. She didn't realize she was falling for him until he fell in love with someone else.

Desperate to get away from her dysfunctional family and avoid the heartbreak of seeing Noah marry another woman, Eden left her hometown, dropped her infamous last name, and built a new life for herself. But when her little sister gets in trouble and pleads for Eden's help, she doesn't hesitate to go back.

Five years after his fiancée dumped him at the altar, Noah has found fulfillment running the youth ministry in his father's church. When a young man under his pastoral care gets a girl pregnant, Noah's there to give guidance and support. He's not prepared to run into the expectant mother's sister, his former best friend Eden, who ghosted him years ago.

Despite past hurts and new feelings, Eden and Noah unite to protect the teen couple from Eden's parents' headline-seeking schemes. But how can they build a future together when Eden can't wait to leave town again and Noah is committed to stay?

ABOUT THE AUTHOR

I write fiction that reflects my Christian faith. I love
happy endings, heroes and heroines who discover
sometimes hard but always vital truths, and stories
that uplift and encourage.
My family and I live in the east of England, where
we enjoy rambling in the countryside, reading good
books and making up silly lyrics to our favorite
songs.
www.millaholt.com

9 781913 416058